NELSON MALONE
SAVES FLIGHT 942

Other Avon Camelot Books by
Louise Hawes

NELSON MALONE MEETS THE MAN FROM MUSH-NUT

LOUISE HAWES lives in Ridgewood, New Jersey, with her children, Robin and Marc. She also wrote *Nelson Malone Meets the Man from Mush-Nut*. About the Nelson Malone books she says: "Nelson helps me remember that silliness can be a nourishing diet and that the best stories, like the best people, are full of curiosity and fun."

NELSON MALONE SAVES FLIGHT 942

LOUISE HAWES

Illustrated by Jacqueline Rogers

AN AVON CAMELOT BOOK

AVON BOOKS
A division of
The Hearst Corporation
105 Madison Avenue
New York, New York 10016

Text copyright © 1988 by Louise Hawes
Illustrations copyright © 1988 by Jackie Rogers
Published by arrangement with Lodestar Books, E.P. Dutton
Library of Congress Catalog Card Number: 87-27257
ISBN: 0-380-70758-6
RL: 6.5

First Avon Camelot Printing: April 1990

CAMELOT TRADEMARK REG. U.S. PAT. OFF. AND IN OTHER COUNTRIES, MARCA REGISTRADA, HECHO EN U.S.A.

Printed in the U.S.A.

OPM 10 9 8 7 6 5 4 3 2 1

to my favorite teachers,
Robin and Marc

Contents

NELSON MALONE SAVES FLIGHT 942

Terrible Tuckman

Nelson Malone was desperate. The first day of school was no time to be without his lucky cap. He'd worn it to the gym on every first day since kindergarten, and if he didn't have it on today, there was no telling whose sixth grade he'd end up in. He might even be assigned to Terrible Tuckman's room.

Ms. Tuckman had a mustache and bright, pink circles on her cheeks. She was bigger than the principal, Mr. Glendinny. She was tougher than James Frackey, the school bully. And she was a lot scarier than the marsh monster in *It Came from the Closet*.

"Could I skip sixth grade?" Nelson tried to sound casual, as if he'd just thought of the idea on his way down to breakfast. Nelson's sister, Robin, wasn't fooled.

"Aren't you a little old to be afraid of the first

day of school?" Robin, who was starting fifth grade, looked very calm and confident. She couldn't have had any butterflies in her stomach, because she was already munching on her second marmalade and egg sandwich.

"I'm not afraid, dum-dum," Nelson explained. "I can't find my baseball cap." He had looked everywhere for the lucky red cap with the eagle clutching a baseball on the visor. He'd searched under his bed, where he kept his hermit crab and all the instant game cards he'd collected for Gino of Genoa's Pizza Palace Sweepstakes. He'd looked in the pile of dirty clothes he'd forgotten to unpack from summer camp. He'd even taken out his dresser drawers in case the hat had gotten pinned behind one of them the way his Scab in Concert T-shirt had.

"I think," Nelson's mother announced as she put a huge plate of toast and eggs at his place, "that skipping sixth grade is a bit drastic." Nelson studied the runny yolk of each egg while his stomach did flip-flops. Ms. Tuckman didn't even allow sneezing without permission.

"As I recall," Nelson's father added, "that hat has seen much better days. Isn't that the one your mother drove the car over last year?"

Mrs. Malone looked uncomfortable. "Yes, I'm afraid so. That was the day we got in the first samples of our new E-Z artichoke steamer. I was planning the introduction to "The A-B-C's of Steaming" and I squashed it flat." Nelson's mother wrote instruction manuals for the E-Z Can Opener Company. She was very involved in her work.

4

"That's okay, Mom. I shouldn't have left it in the garage." Nelson remembered how horrible he'd felt when he found the crushed cap in an oily heap under the right front tire of the station wagon. "Besides, it's not so tight anymore."

"It may *feel* better, Nelson, but I'm afraid your father's right. It doesn't exactly *look* like the first day of school."

"It looks more like the last day of the world." Robin stood up to take her plate into the kitchen. She had a tiny, marmalade-colored stain on the collar of her blouse. "If *I* were your teacher, I'd make you throw that grungy old thing in the trash."

"If you were my teacher, blobhead, I'd learn the same stuff you know, and I'd be the Man with the Invisible Brain!"

For once, Robin didn't try to have the last word. She was in too big a hurry. She raced back into the kitchen, then reappeared with her new book bag in tow. "Melissa and I are walking to school together," she announced, kissing her mother and father.

Mr. Malone seemed disappointed. "But I always drive you the first day. How will you find the right line to stand in?"

"Oh, Daddy, don't be silly. I'm ten years old now!" Robin's two blond ponytails bounced as she shook her head. Each one was wrapped with a blue rubber band the same color as her sweat shirt. Nelson's sister almost always matched.

"Are you sure you and Melissa wouldn't like a ride?" Mr. Malone asked hopefully as Robin was opening the front door.

5

Robin turned around wearing her lemon-tasting face. "Nobody except babies brings their parents to first day," she announced. "Bye, Mommy. Bye, Daddy. Bye, nerdo."

"It looks like it's just you and me, Nelson." Mr. Malone folded his newspaper into a flat square that just fit in his briefcase, and stood up from the table.

"Sorry, Dad," Nelson said, hiding the weepy egg eyes on his plate under a piece of pumpernickel. "Eric's mother is picking me up in five minutes." Eric Lerner was Nelson's best friend. His mother made runny spaghetti sauce and wore fat, squeaky nurse's shoes, but Nelson was sure she wouldn't want to help them find the right line.

"Well, then, I just have to wait until back-to-school night to meet both your teachers." Mr. Malone kissed Mrs. Malone good-bye, then followed Robin out the door. "Have a good first day, Nelson," he called over his shoulder.

But Nelson didn't answer. He was already up to his ankles in one-of-a-kind mittens and old ski hats. By the time his mother found him in the hall closet, he had emptied every shelf. There was no sign of his special cap anywhere.

"What a mess," observed Mrs. Malone, picking through the pile of winter clothes and vacuum cleaner parts. "I guess it's time I threw out some of these things."

Nelson held up a bright blue glove with a red toy soldier knitted into each finger. "You could start with this, Mom," he told her. "I haven't worn it since second grade." He remembered how he used to scrunch his hands together and make believe his ten fingers were fighting a battle. That was before Eric's dog, Woton, had eaten the other glove.

"I'm sorry, Nelson. I'm afraid your cap is really lost. I hope you can get off to a good start anyway." His mother put her arm on his shoulder and looked very understanding. "Now, if you don't need me, I'm going to get back to work on the E-Z kitchen catalogue. I'm already up to the cabbage corer." She pulled a pencil from behind her ear and disappeared upstairs to her office.

Just because your mother does most of her work at home, thought Nelson darkly, doesn't mean you can expect a whole lot of help. I'm about to begin the worst school year of my life, and all Mom can think about is cabbage!

All *Nelson* could think about was Terrible Tuckman. During the ride to school with Mrs. Lerner and Eric, he remembered all the hideous reports he had heard about her from last year's sixth graders. One of them had told him that she hated boys, especially boys with freckles. Lawrence Donovan, who had almost as many freckles as Nelson, said she had made him sit at attention through every recess!

When Eric's mother had dropped the two boys off and they were standing in the middle of the crowded gym, Nelson felt as if he'd eaten a basketball for breakfast. His stomach churned and his throat was dry. He felt so warm that he thought he might be getting a temperature. When he saw Ms.

Tuckman standing at the midcourt line on the gym floor, with a big plastic sign that read 6B, he was *sure* he was getting a temperature.

"Welcome, everybody!" The voice of the school principal thundered across the room. Mr. Glendinny liked to talk loudly anyway, but when he used a microphone, he could reach Alaska. "Welcome to another exciting year at Upper Valley Station Elementary."

Next to Nelson, Eric groaned. "Yeah," he whispered, "as exciting as the chicken pox."

"I won't keep you any longer," the booming voice promised. "I know you're all anxious to get to your new classrooms."

"Yeah," whispered Eric again. "As anxious as turkeys at Thanksgiving."

"Please," begged Nelson, holding his stomach. "Don't talk about food!"

"Now," continued Mr. Glendinny, "if our wonderful teachers will step forward."

"Yeah," began Eric, "as wonderful as . . ."

"Terrible Tuckman," Nelson finished for him. "I know I've got Terrible Tuckman."

"How do you know?" asked Eric. "After all, there are three sixth grades. You might get Ms. Whetmeyer or Mr. Standish."

"No." Nelson stood bareheaded and miserable beside the table where all the students with last names that began with *G* through *P* would meet their teacher. "I couldn't find my lucky cap."

"Oh." Eric was quiet for a minute. "Wait a second," he said at last. "If you get Terrible Tuckman, then so do I! We're always in the same class."

It was true. The two friends were in the same chunk of the alphabet, and they'd been in homeroom together ever since Eric and his parents had moved to Upper Valley Station, New Jersey, four years before. It made things a little easier knowing that Eric, who lived only a few blocks away and always shared his lunch with Nelson when Mrs. Malone packed her special fig and bean sprout sandwich, was going to be in Tuckman's class, too.

"Maybe your mother put your cap in the wash," suggested Eric, who was getting worried. "Did you look everywhere?"

"I sure did," Nelson told him, as Ms. Tuckman walked over to the G through P table. "It's no good. We're doomed."

Ms. Tuckman's eyes were so pale that Nelson couldn't tell if they were blue or brown or any color at all. When she looked at you, you felt just like a rabbit caught in the beam of a flashlight, small and helpless and shaking all over.

"Hello, boys." Her voice was almost as loud as Mr. Glendinny's, and she was staring straight at Nelson's freckles. "Now, let's just check our list to make sure you're in the right place, shall we?"

Nelson didn't need to check. He knew just how bad his luck was going to be. Sure enough, after she had found Nelson's and Eric's names, along with those of the other boys and girls who gathered around the table, Ms. Tuckman smiled a frightening smile. "Yes," she said, the bright, pink circles on her cheeks crinkling as she spoke, "you're all mine!"

Grim and futureless, Nelson and Eric joined the rest of Ms. Tuckman's sixth grade, following her down the green-tiled hall to her classroom. "I have a feeling," Eric whispered to Nelson, "this is going to be as much fun as *The Feast of Dracula.*"

"That was only a *movie,*" Nelson told him as they found two desks at the very back of their homeroom. "This is *real.*"

"Now, Nelson Malone," Ms. Tuckman said from the front of the room, "since you're closest to the door, I'm going to ask you to close and lock it."

Eric looked at Nelson. Nelson looked at Eric. *Lock* it? Behind locked doors, there was no telling what unspeakable things their new teacher planned to do to them! As Nelson walked toward the door, he pictured a whole class full of hypnotized zombies sleepwalking with their hands stretched out in front of them. "Yes, Ms. Tuckman," he mumbled numbly. "Whatever you say, Ms. Tuckman."

Once Nelson had locked the door, Ms. Tuckman seemed to relax. In fact, she giggled right out loud. Then, tiptoeing to the door Nelson had just locked, she turned the handle. When she was sure it wouldn't open, she returned to her desk, reached into a small drawer, and pulled out a flat black box. Next, she walked around her desk and sat on top of it, the package in her broad lap. "I have something to show you," she said in a bright, cheerful voice that didn't sound at all like the one Nelson had heard just a minute ago.

Carefully opening the package, Ms. Tuckman took out a rumpled red something covered with purple and yellow stars. She unfolded the cloth and then wrapped it around her shoulders like a cape. "This is my traveling coat," she announced.

Nelson and his classmates didn't dare say a word. They simply stared at their new teacher, too frightened to move a muscle. Except for Warren Lansdorf, whose nose was always running. Warren took a tissue from his pocket and sniffed as quietly as he could.

"Well," asked Ms. Tuckman, "don't any of you want to know where we're going?" Still no one said anything, and Ms. Tuckman looked disappointed. "Oh, rats and toads, it happens every year!" She sighed and crossed her legs under the red cloak. "If this keeps up, we'll never have time for the House of Horrors."

The back of Nelson's neck felt damp and clammy. Maybe Eric was right, he thought. Maybe this *was* going to be like *The Feast of Dracula.*

"Suppose I were to tell you," the teacher asked her class, "that I'm nothing but a fake? A phony. One hundred percent unnatural. All fillers and added ingredients.

"You see," she whispered confidentially, leaning toward the front row of boys and girls, "there's no such person as Terrible Tuckman." The room got so quiet you could hear Warren sniffling. "There's no one but a little girl named Sylvia Tuckman who hated school as much as you do.

"Now even though Sylvia went to school a long time ago, most of her teachers were just like the ones you have. They worried a lot about teaching their students to say and do the Right Things." Ms. Tuckman's face wore a sad, sweet smile and her pink cheeks shone. "Oh, they meant well enough, you see. It's just that they'd been at it so long, they forgot there's more than one way to teach and lots of ways to learn. Sylvia figured Mrs. Wheatley had been at it forever."

Their teacher stood up, and the red cloak floated around her ankles. "Mrs. Wheatley was Sylvia's third grade teacher. She wore Ben Franklin glasses and had lots of warts. Her whole class was so afraid of giving her 'wrong' answers that they never said a word. That's when Sylvia Tuckman took a solemn oath.

"Sylvia promised herself that she would never forget that there are as many different good answers as there are children. Or snowflakes. Or stars. And she promised herself that she would grow up to be a teacher who never did things the Right Way." Now Ms. Tuckman pulled a puffy, purple bonnet from a pocket in her cape. "And that's precisely what I did!"

Twenty-one pairs of eyes widened and twenty-one mouths dropped open as Ms. Tuckman put the bonnet on and tied the strings under her triple chin. "Of course, I had to infiltrate the system first," she told them. "I had to go to teachers' college and take all the Right Courses and, naturally, I had to get very good grades. Then I had to take a job and pretend to be the sort of teacher grown-ups remember from their school days."

Ms. Tuckman looked nervously at the door as if she thought someone might be listening behind it. "Of course, I'm not that kind of teacher at all. But I had to make certain that no one found out what my students and I really do in class. I had to ask my classes to spread rumors that would keep the principal and parents happy. Rumors about how strict and scary and tough I was." She was still whispering, but there was a wonderful, wicked twinkle in her eyes. "Horrible, terrible rumors that would keep what we do under wraps."

Nelson couldn't stand the suspense. A happy, giddy feeling was building up inside him. "What?" he asked suddenly, jumping up from his seat. "What do we do?"

Ms. Tuckman smiled, walking to the door and quietly unlocking it. "Have fun, of course," she told Nelson. "And we're going to start right now."

Warren Lansdorf sneezed with relief, and Nelson shook Eric's hand. Patty Geldman hugged Tricia Johnson, and a new boy named Harold stood up and cheered. Ms. Tuckman, in her cape and bonnet, laughed right out loud. It was the funniest, tinkliest, most wonderful laugh any of them had ever heard.

"Yes," she told them. "I always like to start school off with a field trip to Huge Adventure Park. It's just the ticket for getting rid of the end-of-summer blahs." She glanced out the window and giggled excitedly. "Goodness, Mr. Phillips has the bus out front already. He's one of my oldest and dearest friends, so he knows all about my secret." She looked solemn for a minute. "Now, remember, until you get on the bus, you must act as if this is the worst, most horrible thing that's ever happened to you. I told Mr. Glendinny I was taking you to the public library to study the Dewey decimal system."

Huge Adventure Park! Nelson and Robin had begged their parents all summer for a trip to the home of the Super-Twister, the longest roller coaster in the world! Before he knew it, Nelson was sitting beside Eric on the bus. It had been hard to walk across the parking lot with a frown on his face when he knew he was headed for the most exciting school day anyone could ever hope for. What a relief when old Mr. Phillips had driven the bus off school property and Nelson was able to look as happy as he felt!

"I can't wait to try the Anti-Gravity Cyclatron!" Ms. Tuckman clapped her hands together in the front seat while Mr. Phillips nodded his bald head and smiled. "Then I think I'll take the House of Horrors ride. Oh, and we can't forget our school supplies. Let me see, we'll all need chocolate pops, cotton candy, and Cracker Jacks. That makes a much better lunch than sandwiches, don't you think?"

The whole class agreed. That's why, as soon as the bus arrived at Huge Adventure, they followed Ms. Tuckman straight to the lake by the Sunken Treasure Boat Ride. She put her fingers up to her mouth and whistled loudly. It was a better whistle than tough James Frackey ever did!

Suddenly every swan and goose on the lake was swimming right up to Ms. Tuckman and her new class. When their teacher counted to three and dropped her hand, Nelson and his classmates started throwing the contents of their lunch bags into the lake. Into the gurgling water went five bologna sandwiches, ten peanut butter and jelly sandwiches, three cream cheese and jelly sandwiches, two tuna sandwiches, and one fig and bean sprout on whole wheat! The swans liked the cream cheese and jelly, the geese liked the bologna, the tuna, and the peanut butter and jelly. The fig and beansprout sandwich floated by itself for a while, then sank softly beneath the surface.

From then on, there was nothing to do but have fun! Ms. Tuckman seemed to have an endless supply of Huge Adventure free passes. "I'm an old and valued customer," she explained as she handed twenty-five passes to each child. "I know there are fewer than twenty-five rides in the park," she told them, "but I really think the Crazy Cars and the Speed Zapper bear repeating."

She was right, of course. Nelson and Eric rode the Zapper right away, and found that, at the top, you felt as if your stomach had relocated to your head and your knees were made of Jell-O. It was terrific!

Even though she had told the class they were on their own until they all met at the Ice-cream Cavern at two o'clock, most of the children wanted to stay with Ms. Tuckman. She was having more fun than anyone, and she knew the ins and outs of every ride. So, while Amy Mangione and Sara Kenner wandered off to look at imprinted T-shirts, the rest of the sixth graders followed their teacher to the guess-your-weight booth. When she broke the scale, the man gave Ms. Tuckman the grand prize, a giant panda bear with a pink ribbon around its neck.

Next, they found the target-shooting games. Eric tried to hit three bull's-eyes and win a glass mirror with a red Ferrari painted on it. He got only one bull's-eye, so the man handed him a puffy yellow heart on a string. "Ugh!" said Eric, who gave the heart quickly to Stacy Henley. "That's for girls."

"I think your left eye was too far open," commented Ms. Tuckman, who had been watching Eric shoot.

"My dad always says to aim with my right eye shut," Eric told her.

"This is the way *I* like to shoot." Ms. Tuckman moved up to the pistol range and stood in front of the target. She gave the man her ticket and then took careful aim. She fired three times and, before they realized what had happened, the children were staring at three black holes in the center of the target. "I'll take the Ferrari, thank you," the teacher told the man behind the counter. He blinked and swallowed hard. Then, without a word, he handed her the mirror with the red car.

"Wow!" Eric's eyes popped when Ms. Tuckman slipped the prize into his arms. He was so surprised and happy, he forgot to say thank you. But Ms. Tuckman didn't even notice. She was too busy studying the Pitch-n-Win booth. It featured four cardboard cats sitting on four brightly colored garbage cans. The idea was to knock all four cats off the cans with five balls. The prizes, arranged on shelves

17

around the booth, included a whole row of baseball caps.

"Look!" cried Nelson suddenly. "My lucky cap!" He pointed to the row of caps and, sure enough, the last cap in the row was a red one with an eagle clutching a baseball sewn on the visor.

Racing to the booth, Nelson handed the man one of his tickets and scooped up five baseballs from the counter. He lined four of them up in a row. Taking the fifth, he wound up, aimed carefully, and let the ball fly toward the first cat, which was perched on an orange garbage can. But his throw was too low, and the baseball landed with a thud beside the can.

He still had four balls left. More carefully now, he wound up again. He put a little twist on the ball and sent one of his special curves straight at the second cat. But this throw was too high, and the ball zoomed into the wall above the cat's left ear and bounced out of the booth onto the dirt floor by Nelson's feet.

He stared at the cap on the shelf. It was exactly like the lucky hat he'd lost. Even though it didn't look as though he could get much luckier than having Ms. Tuckman for sixth grade, he still wanted to win that cap. That's why, after he'd thrown three more balls and knocked down only one of the cats, he gave the man another ticket.

Ms. Tuckman watched Nelson throw five more baseballs and knock down two more cats. As he left the booth, hot and discouraged, to join his classmates, she burst into applause. "Hooray!" she yelled. "A little more top spin and you would have won."

"What?" Nelson already figured Ms. Tuckman was terrific, but he had no idea she liked baseball, too.

"You just forgot to take the wind into account," she continued. "Here. Let me show you what I mean." She stepped up to the counter, gave the man a ticket, and scooped up the five baseballs he handed her. She pulled one from the pile and hurled it toward the first cardboard cat. Without putting the pile of balls down, she threw another and then another. Each ball she threw knocked down the next cat in line until all four garbage cans were empty and she still had one ball left in her hand.

"Holy cow!" exclaimed Nelson as she placed his new lucky cap on his head. "You have a better arm than Dwight Gooden!"

"Not really," replied his teacher modestly. "It's all in the wrist." Carelessly, she wound up with the fifth ball and zoomed it along the floor toward one of the fallen cats. The ball caught the cat just behind its haunches and sent the cardboard shape whirling back up into the air. The boys and girls and the man behind the booth stared in disbelief as the cat landed gently on the same yellow garbage can from which Ms. Tuckman had just knocked it down. "All in the wrist," she repeated, leading her class toward the Ice-cream Cavern.

Amy and Sara found them just as everyone was digging into the Cavern's special, a fabulous float with cookie crumble and three kinds of ice cream. By the time Mr. Phillips drove the bus up to the park gate, Ms. Tuckman's class was as full and happy as any of them could ever remember being. "Now,

don't forget," their teacher warned them on the ride back. "No smiling in the driveway. No laughing in the hall." She grinned as if she couldn't help herself. "You all had a terrible time today and learned a great deal."

"How was your field trip, Ms. Tuckman?" Mr. Glendinny was standing by the front door when they arrived at school. He watched everyone step, frowning and solemn, down the bus steps and trudge, single file, back to the classroom. He had never seen such a quiet, well-behaved group of children.

"Our trip was most instructive, thank you," Ms. Tuckman told him. "We were exposed to a wide variety of learning experiences, and we absorbed massive amounts of educational input."

"That sounds excellent." Mr. Glendinny patted Sara Kenner's head and walked away smiling.

"How was your first day of school?" Robin asked when Nelson got home. She had already beaten him to the refrigerator and was munching on the last piece of cake left over from dinner the night before. Nelson didn't mind a bit.

"Ohhhh," he groaned, putting his hand to his head. "It was a nightmare!" He remembered the Anti-Gravity Cyclatron and the Speed Zapper and the Super-Twister, and tried to keep from smiling. "Terrible Tuckman just never lets up. She's after us every second. Why, she even gave us homework already!"

"On the first day?" Robin stopped eating the cake and started worrying about next year.

"Yep," Nelson said, remembering the Crazy Cars

and the Sunken Treasure Boat Ride and his new lucky cap. "She said that tomorrow we're taking another field trip, so we have to spend tonight going over everything we learned today."

"Gee," said Robin, sounding almost sorry for her big brother. "That's too bad."

"The worst," agreed Nelson, patting the lump that his new lucky cap made in his right front pocket. "The absolute, completely, most horrible worst." Then he stopped and stared at his sister who, except when she was calling him "nerdo," wasn't really too bad. "I just hope *you* get Ms. Tuckman for sixth grade," he told her. "Then you'll know exactly what I mean!"

Halloweenie

Ms. Tuckman made school so exciting that Nelson stopped looking forward to weekends. Sleeping late and walking into town with Eric or playing touch football in Josh Weyman's backyard was all right, but nothing could match the action of 6B! Every week now, Friday meant the end of fun instead of the beginning. It meant Ms. Tuckman's students would have to interrupt their research projects (Nelson was working on a history of skateboards), and all their class pets, including the iguana and the squirrel monkey, would have to go back to the zoo for two days.

That's why Halloween didn't seem very promising. It fell on a Saturday, and Nelson was sure it wouldn't be any fun at all without Ms. Tuckman. Of course, she did her best to get everyone in a spooky, spine-

23

tingly frame of mind with a special Friday matinee at the Upper Valley Cinema. She told Mr. Glendinny that they were going to explore the science of optics. What they really explored was a double feature, *The Thing that Ate Liver* and *Mummy Dearest.* Still, when he got home from school and his mother asked about his costume, Nelson felt strangely detached and uninterested.

"I guess I'll just wear the same thing I did last year," he told her. Then, because he couldn't explain why Halloween had lost its punch without giving away Ms. Tuckman's secret, he added, "I'm getting pretty old to dress up anyway." Mrs. Malone stared at him as he dug into the bottom of the cookie jar. He came up with three pretzels, which he kept, and half a macaroon, which he put back.

"But you've never worn the same costume twice," said his mother. "Every year, you get more sinister." She opened the drawer where she kept string and scissors and stamps. She rummaged through refrigerator magnets shaped like vegetables and a pile of keys that didn't fit anywhere. Finally, she held up a plastic tube with a long red cap. "I even got fresh blood this year." She studied the tube's label, then reported, "Dries in seconds, won't wash off in the rain."

"That's neat, Mom," Nelson said without enthusiasm. "Just the same, I think I'll go as a *ninja* warrior again. Maybe Robin can use the blood."

"I don't think so. She's going as a butterfly."

"Maybe she could be a vampire butterfly," suggested Nelson.

"Maybe you could live in another state," suggested Robin, breezing into the kitchen, throwing her backpack onto the counter, and diving into the cookie jar. "Or another planet," she added, dropping the stale macaroon half back into the jar. "Mom and I already made the prettiest wings in the world, and we don't need your dumb blood messing everything up."

"It's not *my* dumb blood," protested Nelson. "It's Mom's. And I don't know why you always want a pretty costume, anyway. I thought the whole idea of Halloween was to scare people."

"Well," concluded Ms. Malone, "I'm not sure a bloodsucking butterfly is really scary enough to satisfy veteran horror fans. And it certainly isn't the concept I had in mind when I bought this to trim Robin's wings with." She retrieved a second tube from the drawer and handed it to Nelson's sister.

"Oooo!" Robin squealed. "Rainbow glitter! It's perfect, Mom. I'll go get my wings, so we can decide where to put it." She gave the glue tube back to her mother and raced upstairs to her bedroom.

Mrs. Malone, who loved making costumes and decorating them with elaborate designs, looked hopefully at Nelson. "Maybe we could put your initials on your *ninja* costume." She read the label on the glitter tube. " 'This sparkling, easy-to-apply adhesive makes any surface spring to life.' "

"Thanks, anyway, Mom." Nelson turned to follow his sister upstairs. "I think my *ninja* costume has all the spring it needs."

After he had hauled out the long, flat box he kept

under his bed and was pawing through old T-shirts and bathrobes to find his costume, the hall phone rang.

"Hi, Freckle Face," a scornful voice greeted Nelson. "Bet you wimps from 6B can't get more Halloween candy than we can."

It was James Frackey, the biggest boy and the worst bully in the sixth grade. James had lost only one fight, and everyone knew that one didn't count, because it was with Darcy Staples, a girl, and he wasn't really trying.

"Betcha we can, too." Nelson felt almost sorry for James. If he had been in Ms. Tuckman's class, he'd have a lot better things to do than worry about who was going to get the most Halloween candy! In fact, if James hadn't called him "Freckle Face," Nelson might have hung up without adding, "Winner takes all. Deal?"

"Everything?"

"Yep. Even pennies and boxes of raisins."

James didn't sound so sure. "Everything except Malted Mallow Creams. Okay?"

Nelson wasn't going to let James off easy. "Nope," he insisted. "If you win, you take everything we've collected. And if we win, you give us every stick of licorice. Every Mallow Cream. Everything, down to your very last apple. Unless, of course, you don't dare."

"Don't *what*?" Nelson knew James could never resist a dare. It was settled. The contest was on, and Halloween was going to be exciting after all!

26

In a few minutes, Nelson called Eric and told him about the bet. Eric called Shane McCallister, and Shane called Michael Payjack. Michael didn't want to phone any girls, but he got Warren Lansdorf, who thought Sara Kenner was cute, to tell Sara about the challenge from James' class. Pretty soon everyone in 6B was alerted, and all the boys and girls agreed to meet at Nelson's house the next evening.

Mrs. Malone was just helping Robin into her pink tulle wings when Nelson reappeared in the kitchen downstairs. "Maybe I *could* use a bit of that glitter on my costume," he told his mother. He looked at the fluffy, sparkling shapes she was pinning to the shoulders of his sister's pink leotard. "That is, if you haven't used it all up on the Butterfly from the Black Lagoon."

Robin curled her hands up into fists and knotted them on each side of her waist. "You're just jealous because I've got a brand-new costume and you're wearing the same old black pajamas you wore last year."

"Pajamas?" Nelson backed off from the pink butterfly, who could pinch pretty hard when she wanted to. "This is a genuine karate tunic," he told her, waving the black pants and top he'd brought with him. "It's even got a black belt."

"I thought you were too old for dressing up?" Mrs. Malone smiled and rolled the glitter tube all the way up to its gold top. "I think we have enough left to squeeze out an *N* and *M*. Where shall I put them?"

"How about right here?" Nelson stuffed his hand

into a pocket on the shirt of the tunic, while Mrs. Malone dribbled a curly set of initials onto the black cloth. As she traced the tail of the *M*, Nelson noticed that she made a scissors face, sticking her tongue out just like a little kid cutting shapes from paper.

"Thanks, Mom. That looks great." He held the shirt out straight to dry and headed back up to his room. He was halfway up the stairs before he remembered. "Oh, Mom," he called down to her, "would it be all right if I had the kids from my class over tomorrow night?"

Mrs. Malone left Robin and her wings in the kitchen. She ran into the hall, grinning broadly. "A Halloween party? Why, Nelson, you haven't had a Halloween party since you were seven." She put her hand to her forehead, a distant look in her eyes. "Now where *did* I put that Pin-the-Tail-on-the-Black-Cat game? I guess we could use the old, broken hammock in the garage for a spiderweb decoration. And, let's see. Perfect! We'll get your father's camping tent for the spook house."

"Peeled grapes make great eyeballs," announced Robin, who had followed her mother out of the kitchen, leaving a tiny trail of rainbow glitter on the carpet. "And raw hamburger makes terrific squished brains."

"I don't want a spook house," Nelson told them.

"Well, then," asked his mother, "how about Ring-Around-the-Pumpkin?"

"I'm not having a party, Mom."

"But you said—"

"I said I wanted to have the kids in my class over tomorrow." Nelson knew his mother loved to plan parties, but he also knew that beating James Frackey would take a lot more than phony eyeballs and bobbing for apples. "Just for a strategy meeting. We've accepted a trick-or-treat challenge from 6A."

"Oh."

Nelson remembered the orange pumpkin invitations his mother had made for his last Halloween party. And the tiny witches' hats filled with chocolate kisses and candy corn. "Sorry, Mom."

"That's okay, Nelson." Mrs. Malone stooped to pick up some glitter from the rug. "I guess I'm a little old for Halloween parties."

Robin made her lemon-tasting face at Nelson, then hugged her mother. Nelson felt awful. "Maybe we can all stop by for hot chocolate after we win," he suggested.

"That would be nice." His mother brightened. "Should I put gum drops in the marshmallows?"

"Sure," Nelson told her, hurrying upstairs. He hung his *ninja* costume up to dry and slipped the pillowcases off both his pillows. He'd need a lot of room to hold all the candy he was going to collect, and he thought about borrowing a third pillow case from Robin. He studied the roomy cases and then decided that two were probably enough. After all, who would be frightened of a *ninja* warrior carrying a pillowcase covered with flowers and unicorns?

The following night, a strange assortment of gypsies, ape-men, flappers, and pirates started ringing

Nelson's doorbell and filing into the living room. Everyone in his class, except Lisa Gerchner, whose parents didn't let her go out on Halloween, and Miles Mullen, who was always late, had arrived at Nelson's when the meeting began. It didn't get off to a promising start. "I can only be out for two hours," Sara Kenner told her classmates. "And I have to stay within three blocks of this house."

"Me, too," said Amy Mangione. "Plus, my mother says I have to wear a coat, a hat, and mittens over my costume."

"But you're supposed to be a hula girl!" Nelson wondered how anyone was going to be able to tell what Amy was dressed as under the thick red coat and hat she'd placed on the sofa beside her. "Hula girls don't wear mittens!"

Even Eric's costume was a disappointment. He was a pirate again this year, but the silver paint was peeling off his plastic hook, and worse still, his eye patch was white instead of black. "My mom bleached it by mistake," he explained.

"Hey," suggested Warren Lansdorf, who was dressed as a caveman, "if cowboys wear white and black hats, why can't pirates wear white and black patches? Maybe Eric's a good pirate." He slipped a tiny Kleenex package from under his leopard-skin belt and blew his nose loudly.

"Maybe betting with James was a big mistake." Nelson looked around the room. "Do you remember the fantastic costume he wore last year? He was a robot, and his dials really turned and his lights really blinked!"

"My mom wants to inspect my candy before anybody eats it," announced Miles Mullen, as he walked in the door and tried to sit down on a stool beside Eric. He was wrapped from head to foot in silver tinsel, and when he bent his knees, he popped the garland around his waist.

"Who are you supposed to be?" asked Nelson, not at all sure he wanted to hear the answer.

"I'm a Christmas tree, dummy." Miles shook his head, and a tiny gold star attached to his green knit cap twinkled and shook. "Some people don't know anything."

"I know we're in big trouble." Nelson lifted one of Miles' garlands and slowly pushed him onto the stool. "James and his class are supposed to meet us here in five minutes, and we don't even have a plan."

"Well, we can't all stay together," Eric decided. "We'll just have to split up and cover as many houses as we can before Amy and the others have to be home."

"You mean I've got to tell the toughest guy in school that the babies in 6B can't stay out after eight o'clock?" Nelson could just see the giant silver robot's dials whirring as James had a good laugh at them all.

But five minutes later, when the doorbell rang and James appeared at the door, he wasn't laughing at all. He wasn't wearing a robot costume either. He was covered with hair from head to foot and wore a horrible, gruesome mask with pointed teeth and a blood-covered tongue. All in all, James was the most impressive, most revolting werewolf Nelson had ever seen.

"You guys want to give up right now?" James was carrying three pillowcases and standing in front of a horrifying crowd dressed in convict's prison stripes; green monster scales; and black, ominous capes. There wasn't a single hula girl or gypsy in the group. "Well?" roared the werewolf.

"No!" insisted a firm voice behind Nelson. "We won't give up. In fact, we won't lose. We're 6B!" Miles Mullen surprised his whole class by standing up to James. His silver garlands shimmered and his gold star shook, and it was clear that he was one Christmas tree who meant business.

"That's right," added Sara, struggling into her ski parka. "You just go ahead and try to beat us, James Freaky! You haven't got a chance."

Nelson felt pretty proud of his class. They might not be the best dressers, he thought, but they sure knew how to stand up to bullies. "You heard them," he told James. "We're not giving up."

"Okay," said 6A's hairy leader. "Winner takes all, starting right now!" He and his spooky crew spilled out the door and started off down the street. Suddenly, James turned back. "Just one more thing," he growled, waving a dark, menacing claw. "We all have to meet back here by eight o'clock. My mom doesn't want me out more than two hours."

Nelson and Eric watched their classmates take off in different directions, and then decided they would ring a doorbell no one else had thought of. Of

course, the Continental Café didn't actually have a doorbell, but Upper Valley Station's fanciest restaurant was certain to have more people and more luscious snacks in one place than anywhere else in town.

"What a great idea!" Nelson told Eric as they hurried toward Upper Valley Avenue. "I can't wait to see James's face when we come back with chocolate éclairs and cupcakes and cheesecake and . . ."

"Don't forget the after-dinner mints," added Eric, waving his hooked arm as they walked. "They keep them in a big glass bowl by the cash register, and you get to take as many as you want after you've paid the check."

"I like the yellow ones best," Nelson said, remembering the pile of tiny candies his parents had brought back from their anniversary dinner at the Continental this year. "I traded Robin all my white and green ones for her yellows."

"But that means Robin got more, doesn't it?" Eric didn't have any brothers or sisters, only a great big dog named Woton, who licked people's sneakers and chased squirrels.

"Yeah," admitted Nelson. "But the green ones taste like cough drops."

"Well, don't be picky tonight, Nelson. Just grab as many as you can."

"*If* they let us in." Now that they were standing in front of the big brick building with its polished brass door, Nelson wasn't so sure their plan would work. He peered through a window and saw lots of men and women eating at tables covered with pale pink tablecloths. The tinkle of the diners' glasses and the murmur of their talking didn't come through the glass, so it was like watching a movie with the sound turned off.

"They *do* look pretty busy," agreed Eric, his elbows resting on the window ledge beside Nelson's. "Maybe we should try somewhere else."

"No!" insisted a third figure, who joined the boys at the window and peered in through the glass. "I like this place. I want to go in."

Nelson was surprised to find a tiny trick-or-treater next to them on the sidewalk. "Where did you come from?" he asked the little fellow, who was sporting a ghost costume, or rather a ragged sheet, that was much too long for him. Its tattered edges were dragging along the ground and already covered with dirt. "Where's your mom?"

"I'm not with my mom," answered the baby spook. "I'm with you big guys." He waved his orange-handled flashlight, blinding both boys with its bright beam.

"Oh, great," Eric told Nelson. "This is all we need. A tagalong from the kindergarten set!"

"I don't go to kindergarten." The little, torn sheet shook indignantly and folded its arms around the flashlight. "Boooo!"

"Yowee zowee." Eric laughed. "You're scaring me to death, little guy. Come on, Nelson. We better get away from you-know-who, or we'll never beat 6A." Quickly he pushed open the heavy brass door and slipped inside the restaurant.

Nelson hesitated a moment. He looked down at

the ghost, who was no taller than a five year old. The little fellow turned to him, his round eye holes sagging and black. "Look, Pee Wee," explained Nelson, "if you're going to go out on Halloween, you better learn something about being scary. First of all, real spooks never say boo."

"They don't?" The tiny tot's voice sounded wobbly and uncertain, as if he might cry.

"Of course not. In *The Thing that Ate Liver*, all the undead hold their hands out in front of them and moan. Try it." Nelson held his arms out stiffly and wailed, "I am a spectral shape come to seek vengeance on your kin."

Pee Wee poked his sheet out in front of him, held back his head, and squeaked, "I am a speckled ape come to eat veggies on your chin."

"No, no, no!" Nelson shook his head, hardly able to keep from laughing. "You've got it all wrong. Maybe we better try another movie. In *Mummy Dearest*, there are three crypt monsters. Of course, they're a lot bigger than you, but they *are* wrapped in white sheets like yours. Best of all, they don't moan too much. Just hold up one of your arms like it was broken." Nelson demonstrated by hanging his left arm out awkwardly and swinging it from the elbow. "Okay. Now walk very slowly, like your feet were glued to the floor, and say, 'May the curse of Dundar follow you to your grave.'"

Pee Wee, trying his best to limp the way Nelson showed him, took a deep breath and yelled as loudly as he could, "May the purse of Dumbo swallow your cave."

Nelson gave up. The little guy just didn't have a scary bone in his body. "It's no good, Pee Wee," he said. "I'm afraid you'll never make a good ghost. Maybe you better go find your mom. I have to catch my friend." He hurried into the restaurant, closing the big door behind him before the tagalong could squeeze inside. He felt a little guilty as he glanced over his shoulder and saw Pee Wee peering in through the window. "Go on. Go home," he said, even though he knew the toddler couldn't hear him through the glass. Finally, he settled for waving a great big good-bye and went to find Eric.

Inside the Continental, there was soft piano music playing and a very tall man in a black jacket towering over Eric. He had barred the way into the bright dining room, where all the men and women were eating. "I'm sorry," he was saying, "we don't allow trick-or-treaters."

"May the purse of Dumbo swallow your cave," said a small voice by Nelson's elbow.

Nelson spun around and, sure enough, there was Pee Wee. "How did you get in here so fast?" he asked, wondering how the tyke had managed to push open the heavy brass door.

"Why did you bring *him* in here?" Eric asked Nelson.

The tall man bent down to Pee Wee. "Well, hi there, little tyke," he said, patting the torn sheet. "What's that about Dumbo?"

"Boo!" Pee Wee stuck out one of his tiny arms and swung it from the elbow. "My arm is broken," he explained.

Nelson groaned, but the tall man smiled and winked broadly at Nelson and Eric. "In that case," he said, "I guess it's safe to let you do a little bit of trick-or-treating after all. How much candy can you take with just one arm, right?" He held back his head and laughed for a long time. Then he straightened up and looked at Nelson and Eric. "All right, boys. I guess you and your little brother can come get a treat from Chef Henri in the kitchen. I'll lead the way."

Eric was furious. "But he's not our . . ."

"I'm not their brother," Pee Wee told the tall man as the three of them followed him into the tinkling dining room, right past a beautiful lady in a long white dress who was playing the piano. "I'm a crypt monster."

"And the cutest little monster I ever saw," said the beautiful lady, who stopped playing and handed Pee Wee some chocolate candy from a glass dish on top of the piano. Pee Wee put the candy up to his sheet but stopped where there should have been a mouth hole. Clearly, he couldn't eat the treat without taking off his costume.

"Here, take one of my pillowcases," Nelson told him. "You can eat it later." He handed the little guy the case and helped him drop in the candies.

"And here's some for you, too, boys." The lady poured the rest of the candy into Nelson's and Eric's pillowcases and then began to play the piano again. "Bye-bye."

"Maybe it's a good thing you let the kid in, after

all," Eric admitted as they followed the tall man past more tables.

"I'm not a kid," Pee Wee insisted, as he rushed by a table where ten people were eating a huge chocolate cake with three layers and white frosting. "I'm an undead."

"Oooo," squealed one of the women at the table. "Isn't he adorable?"

"Yes!" agreed another woman at the same table. "Let's give the little ghost some of Jack's birthday cake."

A fat man with a red mustache, who must have been Jack, laughed. "Well, it's my birthday, but it's also Halloween. Why not?" He wiped a knife with a thick cloth napkin and then cut a slice of the chocolate cake. "And here's two for your brothers," he added, cutting two more slices. "Can you have these wrapped for the boys?" he asked the tall man.

"Certainly, sir," replied the tall man, bending a little at the waist and accepting a plate with the three cake slices on it. "Now, come along, boys."

"I'm not a boy!" protested Pee Wee, as he followed the man into the kitchen, past the cooks in white aprons, right up to the head chef, Henri. "I'm a speckled ape."

"Aha! Eet ees a coincidence," said Henri, whose voice was very loud and whose apron was covered with raspberry-colored stains. "I 'ave 'ere in zees box some verrry special treats for leetle monkeys."

"I've come to eat veggies on your chin," wailed Pee Wee, walking around the kitchen as if his feet

39

were glued to the floor. When Henri caught up with him and handed him the box, Eric couldn't resist peeking inside.

"Wow!" Eric lifted the lid while Nelson and Pee Wee stared into the box. There, nestled in waxy, white tissue paper were ten terrific French pastries. There were éclairs, and tiny cakes, and pies with fruit and shiny glaze all over them. There was even a lemon tart with a clown's face made of sugar right on top.

Nelson knew a winning technique when he saw one. "I'm a speckled ape, too," he told Henri.

"You loook more like a *neenja* warrior to me," observed Henri, rubbing a greasy hand under his chin. "But, I suppose *neenja*s need to eat, too!" He handed Nelson a box almost as big as the one he had given Pee Wee.

"What about pirates?" asked Eric. "We get awfully hungry sailing the bounding main."

"'Ere you are, *mon capitaine.*" Eric got a box, too, and, when he lifted his eye patch to look inside, he let out a little yelp of delight. "I don't know what they are," he told Nelson in a happy daze, "but there are at least a dozen of them, and they're covered with chocolate syrup and marshmallow candies!"

"'Appy 'Alloween!" Henri waved as the three boys followed the tall man out of the kitchen and back through the dining room. Before they reached the front door, though, more diners had dropped desserts and mints into their treat bags.

"What a darling little ghost!" the women all cooed.

"There you go, buddy," said one man, dropping two dollar bills and a cream puff wrapped in a napkin into Pee Wee's pillowcase.

"You sure are some spook," a young man with a bright purple vest told Pee Wee. "Don't scare my girlfriend." He put his arm around a plump, pretty girl sitting beside him and fished a candy bar and two packs of chewing gum from his pockets.

"Oh, he doesn't scare me," his girlfriend told him. She opened her pocketbook and took out a bag of hard candies wrapped in colored plastic. "I think he's a dear."

"May the purse of Dumbo . . ." began Pee Wee, but the tall man wouldn't let him finish. He hurried the boys toward the door, helping Pee Wee lug his swollen pillowcase. The bulging bag looked as if it might explode, and even Nelson's and Eric's cases were filled to the top.

"I think it's just about your bedtime, young fellow," the man said, bending down to shake Pee Wee's hand through the sheet.

"Crypt monsters don't sleep," grumbled Pee Wee as he followed Nelson and Eric out the big brass door and onto the street. "I've come to eat veggies."

"Vengeance," corrected Nelson. "You're supposed to seek vengeance. Can't you get anything right?"

"Hey," Eric told him. "Leave the little guy alone. He did just fine. In fact," he added, stopping to peek inside his treat bag, "I've never seen so much great stuff. I even got a candle from the birthday cake!"

"Yeah," agreed Nelson, opening his own pillowcase and running his hands through the pile of candy and cakes. "I guess old James is going to be sorry he ever took *us* on!"

"Oh, my gosh!" Eric looked at the watch strapped above his plastic hook. "It's almost eight o'clock. We better get back to your house, Nelson."

"Yes, Nelson," echoed Pee Wee. "We better get back."

"Now, look," warned Eric. "Your bringing you-know-who into the restaurant worked out okay, but we better find his parents fast and get out of here."

"I don't have any parents." Pee Wee tripped over his sheet and landed on the sidewalk. Nelson helped him pick up his treat bag and flashlight. "I'm undead."

"Yeah," Eric laughed. "And I'm Defendo, the Galactic Warrior!" He looked up and down the empty street. "Why would anyone let a little kid like this go out by himself?"

"I'm not a little kid."

"Come on, Pee Wee." Nelson had made up his mind. James Frackey or no James Frackey, they had to find the tiny trick-or-treater's parents. "I don't care if it takes all night. We're going to find your mom and dad."

He grabbed Pee Wee's hand under the sheet and started off down the street. But they'd only gone a few blocks when their path was blocked by a ferocious werewolf and two green-eyed vampires. "It looks like you could use a little help carrying all that candy," snarled James, standing so close to them that Nelson could feel James's nylon fur against his cheek. "Let us give you a hand."

Before Nelson could say a word, or even move a muscle, the two vampires had grabbed his bag of treats and were pawing through it. "Hey, look at this," yelled one. "They got chocolate éclairs!"

"And lady fingers! And butterscotch cupcakes!" The other vampire now stepped over to Eric. "I wonder if he's got some some stuff he need. help with, too."

"Let's find out." James chuckled and waved a hairy claw under Eric's chin. "You wouldn't think of not sharing with your friends now would you, Lerner?"

Nelson dropped Pee Wee's hand and faced James. "Hey," he said, "that's no way to win a contest."

"All right," growled James. "Let's keep things fair." He folded his shaggy arms and snorted a wolf laugh. "You and your little friend can be on Lerner's side, and we'll play Finder's Keepers." The vampires howled their approval and again closed in on Eric's bag.

Suddenly, though, James spotted Pee Wee's bulging sack. "Wait just a minute!" he yelled as Eric yanked his bag out of a vampire's clutches. "Small fry here has twice as much as they do." He reached over and opened one side of the little tyke's bag to reveal a mass of dollar bills, coins, and rich desserts. "Golly!" he gasped, forgetting to use his deep, werewolf voice. "This baby's got enough candy to last us all for months! Look, he's even got a whole lemon meringue pie in here!"

The vampires raced over to peer in Pee Wee's bag, while the tattered sheet trembled furiously. "I am NOT a baby!" yelled Pee Wee at last. "May Dumbo's cave swallow your veggies!"

Nelson couldn't stand to see the three big kids picking on Pee Wee. "Look, Frackey," he told the bully, "if you leave the little guy alone, 6B will forfeit the contest. How's that?" He put his arm around the tiny figure in the sheet. But he could hardly hold on, because Pee Wee was bouncing up and down, his flashlight waving and his treat bag flopping.

"I am NOT a little guy! I eat liver!"

"Sure, sure," agreed Nelson, patting Pee Wee and turning to James. "One thing is for sure, Frackey. This kid is not in our class, and he's not part of the contest. So let him go and leave his candy alone!"

"Says who?" asked James, who remembered to use his werewolf voice this time.

Nelson swallowed. James was a really good fighter. Nelson wasn't. "Says me, that's who."

"And me," added Eric, standing beside his friend. Nelson's heart sank. Eric was a good kicker, but that meant he never got started until after he'd been knocked down. And once James Frackey knocked you down, you usually stayed down.

"And me," joined in Pee Wee, who had stopped whirling and jumping and stood between Nelson and Eric.

The three of them sticking together seemed to make James madder than ever. "Hey, if you think I'm going to let a pint-sized kid in a sheet tell me what to do, you're crazy!" He started tugging on Pee Wee's sack, but he couldn't wrestle it from the little fellow's grasp.

"I'm not a kid!" Pee Wee was beginning to jump up and down and wave his flashlight again. Suddenly his sheet got caught under someone's feet, and he hit the pavement with a thud. His orange flashlight clattered to the ground where it cast a bright beam right onto James' angry face. "Boo!"

"Gee, junior," said James with a sneer, his red face lit up like a jack-o'-lantern. "I'm so scared I'm shaking! Why, under that sheet I bet you're wearing a big, bad diaper, aren't you?" With that, he tugged as hard as he could on Pee Wee's sheet, pulling it off with one swipe of his ugly, black claws.

The sheet came away in James' hands, but there was no kindergartner left on the sidewalk. In fact, to everyone's astonishment, there was no one at all. Unless you counted the faint, shimmering cloud that bounced up and down like a shadow in the air. "I'm not a baby," came Pee Wee's voice from the middle of the dancing cloud. "I'm a GHOST!"

Nelson looked at Eric. Eric looked at Nelson. James and the vampires looked at the strange, misty shape that began to move toward them. Suddenly a horrible scream pierced the night air. It was James, yelling at the top of his lungs and running as fast as he could down the street and out of sight. Behind him, the two vampires struggled to keep ahead of the small cloud of mist that pursued them into the distance.

Eric stopped to retrieve his pillowcase. The vampires had dropped his and Nelson's candy as soon as they'd seen what wasn't under Pee Wee's sheet. Beside the three bags that Nelson, Eric, and Pee Wee had collected, lay three more bags, not quite as full. "Looks like James and his friends didn't really want their candy," Eric said, handing Nelson some of the loot.

Nelson opened one of the vampire's bags and found three gift certificates for the Ice-cream Palace. "I guess they didn't care too much about this contest, after all," he observed, glancing down the street to where the three had disappeared. "We said winner takes all, and they left everything for us."

"Yeah, but what about *this* bag?" Eric held up Pee Wee's pillowcase, brimming with luscious pastries and shiny coins.

"Well," ventured Nelson, remembering the way the little cloud had streaked after James and the vampires, "I'm not sure whether or not ghosts can eat." He took the bulging case from Eric and placed it beside the orange flashlight, which was still sending its bright beam skyward. "But I do know Pee Wee earned every last treat in this bag, and I think we should leave it here for him. Besides," he added, scooping up a yellow after-dinner mint and tucking it back into the ghost's bag, "this candy might be haunted."

Slam

6B decided to celebrate their Halloween victory with Ms. Tuckman. They divided up the mounds of candy that 6A dropped off at Nelson's house and brought all the bags to school on Monday. Sara and Amy decorated the classroom with orange and black streamers, and Lisa Gerchner, who had the biggest record collection in the sixth grade, put her newest rock album on the phonograph.

"I don't believe I've ever seen so much candy in one place at one time," said Ms. Tuckman, smiling broadly as the music blared and the children piled the bags of treats in front of her desk. She cupped her chin with one plump hand and studied the bulging paper bags and pillowcases. "Yes, I think you've got enough to roll in."

"To what?" asked Eric, who couldn't wait to start eating. "I thought you were going to pass it out."

"Well, I could do that," admitted Ms. Tuckman, opening one of the bags, taking out a Twizzle Pop, and twirling it between her fingers. "I just hate to disappoint little Sylvia Tuckman, though. You see, she always dreamed of having a mountain of candy to roll in."

"Of course!" Nelson remembered how he had loved jumping into piles of fall leaves when he was tiny. He remembered the delightful rustling and crackling under, over, and all around him. He raced to the front of the room where Ms. Tuckman was already pouring a bagful of candy onto the floor. Standing beside her, he turned another one of the bags over and watched the colorful wrappers fall to the floor.

"*Eeee* electric baby," sang the voice on the stereo, "you give me a charge." Then, as the music got faster, all the students jumped up from their seats and started turning their treat bags upside down, too. "Uncross your wires, and let me plug into your heart," cried the singer, while the heap of candy in front of Ms. Tuckman's desk grew larger and larger. When it was as high as the blackboard and Lisa's record was at its very loudest, Ms. Tuckman raised one hand. "On the count of three," she yelled happily. "One. Two. Three!"

As the drums pounded and the electric guitar whined, all the children jumped or dive-bombed or fell onto the mountain of Halloween candy. They jostled and tumbled up to their ears in chocolate

bars. They crinkled and crackled and rolled in candy corn and chewing gum and malted milk balls. They pelted one another with popcorn; they buried one another in taffy and licorice and wafers. The heap of candy was so gigantic that even Ms. Tuckman, who was by now a lot bigger than little Sylvia Tuckman, succeeded in hiding under a pile of gumdrops and jelly worms.

"I blew my fuse when you turned me down." The song was the latest hit by Nelson's favorite rock group, Slam. As he sank into a sea of chocolate kisses and watched the children around him wading in candy, Nelson was sure he'd never been happier. "I've got electric blues and that's a jolt," wailed Slam's lead singer, Fuzz. "Your kisses feel like 500 volts. Weeeee-oooooo. Weeeee-oooooo."

"This is an awesome album," Nelson told Lisa when he found her under the sour balls. "I think Drool is possibly the greatest musical genius alive today." Daniel Drool was Slam's drummer and song-writer. Nelson had written him at least ten fan let-ters. (Ten and a half if you counted the postcard he'd sent to Slam fan headquarters to tell them he'd never received his personally autographed photo of Drool.) "Of course, he isn't just raw talent, either. He wears terrific makeup."

"Drool's all right," agreed Lisa, unwrapping an or-ange sour ball and popping it into her mouth. "But it's Fuzz and Bryan Weird I can't wait to see this weekend."

"This weekend?" Nelson sat up, kisses and candy

corn showering from his shoulders. "You mean Slam is coming to town this weekend?"

"Of course." Lisa tossed her stringy red ponytail. "They're giving a concert at Upper Valley Stadium, and my brother got two tickets yesterday."

"He did?" Nelson had never seen Slam in person. In fact, he'd never gotten a reply to any of his letters to Drool. (Unless you counted the printed card from fan headquarters that said, "Slam wishes we could respond personally to your kind letter. Your autographed photo will arrive under separate cover. Rock on, Daniel Drool." Nelson had waited and waited. He looked under every separate cover that had arrived, including all his mother's seed catalogs, the electric bills, even the letter from Yvette Bernaise, Robin's French pen pal. But the autographed picture never came.)

"I bet we got the last tickets, too," Lisa told him proudly. "Slam's concerts are always sellouts. Grover and I are going to have to sit way at the back of the stadium, but I don't care." She sighed, rolled the sour ball into her right cheek, and closed her eyes. "Just to hear Fuzz's dreamy voice in person is worth it!"

"Yeah," admitted Nelson glumly. "I sure wish I were going." Even if there were still some tickets left, though, his chances of getting one were slim. He had just borrowed three week's allowance from Robin to buy a laser turret for his Tower of Doom collector's set. Before she shook the money from her china clown bank, she had made him promise not

51

only to pay her back, but also to let her watch "Love Yacht" every Friday night for the rest of the year. He had nothing left to give!

"Too bad you have to miss it," Lisa told Nelson, standing up as the record ended. "Slam's going to wear white body suits and bounce a light show off their chests." She stood up, brushing a green jelly worm from her skirt. "Did you know the Fuzz-guitar glows in the dark?"

The Fuzz-guitar was Fuzz's famous purple over-sized guitar. Slam claimed it was the world's largest electric guitar, and critics claimed it was the loudest. Nelson would have given all the candy he was sitting in just to see it.

But he was sure it would do no good to ask his parents for money to buy a ticket to Slam's concert. He remembered their reactions to the group's latest video, "Pizza Dreams."

"Why is he playing the drums standing on his head?" Mrs. Malone had asked, a confused, apprehensive tone in her voice, as she watched Drool.

"Is there a story line here?" Mr. Malone had wanted to know. "I mean what did that girl with the purple hair do to make the band so mad at her?"

"They're not mad at her, Dad," Nelson had explained without taking his eyes from the television screen. "They're just spray painting a face on her Camaro."

"Do you have any idea what that's going to do to the finish on that poor girl's car, Nelson?" Mr. Malone had shaken his head and headed for the kitchen. He turned back toward the screen as he reached the doorway. "And look at that fellow with the silver sunglasses. He didn't even ask if everybody wanted pepperoni."

No, Nelson decided. It was no use asking his mother and father for help. Discouraged, he slumped into his desk and chewed a Twizzle Pop while Ms. Tuckman gave out the assignments for the next day. Everyone was supposed to choose a partner and walk into town to use up the Halloween gift certificates they'd collected. Amy and Sara chose two Gino of Genoa's coupons for a slice with extra cheese. Warren and Miles decided to redeem the Ice-cream Palace certificates. And Eric and Nelson each took a Simpson's Stationery coupon redeemable for one dollar's worth of merchandise.

"Don't you know," Eric asked as they walked into town after school, "that Simpson's just gives people these coupons so they'll come into the store and spend more money?"

Nelson reached into his pockets and came out with two sticks of strawberry-flavored bubble gum and a tiny plastic rocket from an old Converto-bot that used to turn from a jeep into a launching pad before he'd lost most of the pieces. "I don't have any money at all," he told his friend. "How much have you got?"

Eric frowned and dug into both front pockets of his jeans. He found a nickel, two rubber bands, and a note he'd forgotten to bring home announcing back-to-school night. Then he frowned again and squeezed into his back pockets. He found another nickel and a faded blue tag that said 100% Cotton,

Machine Wash Warm, Tumble Dry Medium, Remove Promptly. "I've got ten cents," he said at last.

"Then I guess neither of us has much to worry about, do we?" Nelson gave Eric a stick of gum, and they both headed for Simpson's, blowing bubbles as they went. But before they reached the store, they found themselves surrounded by a big crowd of people a few blocks up the street. As the two boys got closer, they saw what seemed like hundreds of excited teenagers jostling and pushing each other in an effort to reach the Valley Rest Hotel. But it was no use. If any of the youngsters broke through the barricades that had been set up across the street, a huge policeman and two burly men in brown suits barred the way to the front door.

"Wow! What's going on?" Nelson felt himself whirled this way and that as the boys and girls around him rushed toward the hotel.

"Haven't you heard?" asked a skinny, dark-haired girl as she dashed past him. "That's where Slam is staying."

"They're already here?" Nelson watched the skinny girl race off and disappear into the crowd. "I thought the Slam concert wasn't until this weekend."

"It's not," shouted a tall boy with glasses, who had to hold onto Nelson's shoulder to keep from being pushed ahead by the crowd. "They're in town to film a new video." The boy stood panting next to Nelson and Eric for a moment, then let himself be shoved back into the stream that headed for the hotel. "They're shooting it at Zeinhoffer's Junkyard," he yelled as he was swept out of sight.

"Zeinhoffer's Junkyard!" Nelson and Eric stared at each other in disbelief. The most outrageous, famous rock group in the country was filming a video right in their home town! And staying at the Valley Rest! Both boys looked longingly at the old hotel. It towered above them, its twenty stories soaring into the sky. From behind which one of the countless windows were Drool and Fuzz and Bryan Weird peering out onto the street below?

"We've just *got* to meet them!" Nelson thought of the way his rock idol shook his shaggy mane and sneered, the way he crouched down on the floor to play the bottom of his drums. "Drool rules! Drool rules! Drool rules!" Nelson yelled.

Pretty soon the boys and girls around them had taken up Nelson's chant and, screaming "Drool rules!" they closed in on the policeman and the brown-suited men at the front door of the hotel. Then, as the chanting got louder and louder, Nelson grabbed Eric's elbow, ducked down and crawled out of the yelling crowd on his hands and knees.

"What did you do that for?" asked Eric as he felt himself pulled away from the action. "Three people stepped on me. Besides, we were almost up to the door."

"But it's the *wrong* door," Nelson explained as he led Eric around the block to the back of the hotel. "No one will ever get in the *front* door. They've got it too well guarded."

"Hey!" Eric clapped Nelson on the back as they stumbled past garbage cans and parked cars and at last came to a small, green metal door with no handle. "You're right, there's no one watching this door at all!"

Both boys raced for the door and began to tug with all their might. But, because there was no handle to grab, the door remained firmly shut. "No wonder they aren't guarding this door," Nelson said at last, panting. "It must only open out."

Just as he said this, the door flew open, pinning Eric and Nelson behind it. Two young men with long hair and tight jeans rushed outside and strode toward the parking lot. As the boys held their breath, they watched the men unlock a white van, open the back, and take out a huge speaker and a set of drums. Then, as quickly as they'd appeared, the men walked back inside, carrying the speaker and drums and letting the door close behind them.

Without a word, Nelson and Eric walked over to the van. Sure enough, the silver letters across its side announced, SLAM PRODUCTIONS. The back doors of the truck, which the men had forgotten to close, hung open on their hinges, revealing a tangle of wires, boxes, and instrument cases. On the face of the biggest guitar case they'd ever seen was printed the word *Fuzz*.

"Wow!" Eric's eyes were round with excitement. "This is Slam's van!"

"And that's the Fuzz-guitar!" Nelson couldn't resist

jumping into the van to touch the giant leather case. It was a deep violet color with two gold clasps that sparkled in the dark.

"And this must be Bryan's synthesizer!" Eric hopped in beside Nelson. He closed the door behind him, then stooped to caress a long, rectangular box just the right size for a keyboard. *Weird* was spelled out in flowing gold letters along its side.

Nelson and Eric were so busy exploring the contents of the van that the two men were halfway across the parking lot before the boys heard them coming. "Oh, no!" Nelson watched Slam's roadies getting closer and closer through the little window at the rear of the van. "They're coming back. What'll we do?"

Eric looked around the van. Suddenly he dashed over to the guitar case and opened the lid. The case was empty. He crawled inside and closed the lid over his doubled-up body. "Quick, Nelson!" he urged from under the black velvet lining of the case. "Hide!"

Nelson tried the synthesizer case, but when he pried open the top, he found a big keyboard inside with hardly enough extra room for sheet music!

He heard the handle of the van door turn. His heart was beating as loud as Drool's drums! The handle stopped moving as the men outside began to argue. "I carried those drums up fourteen flights of stairs," insisted one gruff voice. "I ain't carryin' the keyboard, too."

Nelson tried to duck under a pile of wires, but the

slender cables just slipped off him, leaving him without a hiding place.

"Well, if you think haulin' that speaker was any picnic," replied another, deeper voice, "you're crazy."

Desperate, Nelson knocked on Fuzz's guitar case. "Eric," he whispered. "Open up!"

Eric peeped out from the case. "Let me in," insisted Nelson, putting one foot into the case beside Eric.

"I can't." Nelson could hardly hear Eric. His arms were curled against his face and his knees were drawn up under his chin. He looked like a human hedgehog balled up inside the cramped case. "There isn't any room."

"Okay, okay," grumbled one of the men outside the van. "Have it your way. I'll take the keyboard." The door with the tiny window began to open.

"Move over!" Nelson was frantic. Just as the door swung wide, he squeezed and wedged and stuffed himself into the guitar case beside the human hedgehog. He could feel Eric's sneaker right under his nose and hear a muffled protest as his own heel dug into his friend's stomach. "Sorry," he apologized, reaching up to close the lid over them just as the roadies climbed into the van.

Before they knew it, the boys heard the clasps on the guitar case snap shut and felt themselves being lifted up and bumped from side to side as the men carried the rest of Slam's equipment up to the group's hotel suite. "Boy!" complained the man who had won the argument. "I thought they saved these

58

fancy cases for shows. But the Fuzz-guitar's gotta be in here. This thing's heavy as a rock!"

"Yeah," sympathized the other man. "Hauling anything up these stairs is rough. I sure wish the elevators were working."

So did Nelson and Eric. With every step, the guitar case slammed into one of the men's legs or against the wall. The boys were pitched against each other and dashed into the sides of the case. By the time they reached the fourteenth floor of the hotel, they were too dizzy and bruised to be proud of their accomplishment.

It wasn't until the guitar case was resting quietly on the floor beside a table where Drool, Fuzz, and Bryan Weird were finishing lunch, that the boys realized they were in Slam's hotel suite! They had actually succeeded in reaching the rock idols that hundreds of boys and girls in the street below could only dream of meeting!

"Well," announced a deep, rich voice that Nelson recognized instantly as Fuzz's, "you've really outdone yourself this time, Drool, old buddy." There was a scraping sound as a chair moved back and someone stood up from the table. "I think 'Flat Tire, Full Heart' is our best song yet."

"You're right, mate," came the enthusiastic, not very humble answer. "It does set a new standard, doesn't it?" Jammed inside the case, breathing the heady aroma of Eric's sneaker, Nelson trembled to think he was actually listening to Daniel Drool in person.

A second chair scraped and someone else stood up

from the table. "What do you say," a new voice suggested, "we run through it once? I still don't understand the sound you want after the last verse, Drool."

There seemed to be very little air left inside the guitar case. Nelson felt his mouth opening and closing as if he were a stranded fish gulping for breath.

Finally the third chair was scraped away from the table and Nelson listened to the band opening the boxes of equipment the roadies had brought up. No one approached the guitar case, though, and soon Slam was practicing their new, still-to-be-released song, never guessing two of their young fans were so nearby. Even in his miserable, upside-down prison, Nelson thrilled as the soft strum of an unplugged electric guitar and the rhythmic pulse of the electronic keyboard reached him. Soon Drool's unmistakable drumbeat was added, and Nelson knew he was hearing history.

"She was standing by the road. I pulled off to one side. Eoyoooow." Fuzz sang the words to Drool's latest composition while the band played on. "Hey, pretty mama, can I give you a ride? Eoyoooow." Eric must have been having trouble breathing, too, because with every downbeat, the sneaker under Nelson's chin jerked and ·kicked. Nelson tried to back his head away, but there was no room to escape.

"Her tire was flat, but her lips were round. Eoyoooow." Drool's drums grew more feverish, reaching a sonorous crescendo that sent Eric's sneaker right into Nelson's nose. Nelson felt a terrible, tre-

mendous sneeze build up inside him as he inhaled the rubber sole. "Hey, Easy Rider, don't let it get you down. Eoooyoooooow."

"Sweet road runner, let's stay right here," sang Fuzz, his voice climbing as Drool's drums pounded. "You got my motor in racing gear. Eeeeeeeoyo-wieeeee." Nelson held his breath and tried not to think about the sneaker.

"Now your tire is fixed, and you've left too soon. Eoyoooow. I'm standing here, baby, just breathing your fumes. Eeeeoyoooowieeeiieee."

Nelson couldn't hold the sneeze in any longer. He knew that as soon as they were discovered, Slam would call their bodyguards, and he and Eric would have to leave. Still, as the song came to an end and Eric's sneaker ground into the tip of his nose, he had no choice. "AAAAAAACHOOOOOOOO!" Eric's foot gave one final kick before the guitar case popped open, and both boys tumbled out onto the floor, blinking in the light. Slam and their fans stared at one another in stunned silence for only a moment before Nelson exploded once more. "AAAAAAAAACHOOOOOOOOOOOOOOOOOOOO!"

"That's it!" Drool, a shock of his curly dark hair falling across one eye, thumped his chest and then began to laugh. "It's perfect!" he chortled, dancing around the boys. "Do it again!"

"Do what?" asked Nelson, surprised that his idol hadn't already sent for his bodyguards.

"Make that sound you just made. That wonderful, fantastic, slam-bang sound!" Drool picked up his drumstick and repeated the last few bars of his new song. "There," he announced, grinning so widely that a silver filling gleamed and winked at the boys. "There's where it belongs. It's just the sound we need after the last verse!"

Eric looked at Nelson. Then he looked at Drool and Fuzz and Weird. "All Nelson did was sneeze," he explained. "He couldn't help it."

"That wasn't just a sneeze," crowed Drool, turning now to the other members of the band. "That was an explosion. That was the end of a tire and a lover's dreams. That was the end of the world, of desire, of ideals. That, mates, was the finish for our new song!"

Bryan Weird smiled a crooked little smile. He cocked his blond, crew-cut head to one side while he thought things over. "You know," he admitted, "I think you've got something, Drool. There was a sort of primitive energy, a kind of—"

"Finality," interrupted Fuzz. "That's what Drool's been trying to tell us all along." He stared in wonder at the two boys, his arms still draped around the huge purple guitar in his lap. "Without even knowing it, these kids have found the sound we need."

"So, what do you say, munchkins?" Drool put his hands on his hips and grinned again at Nelson and Eric, who stood up slowly and looked around the bright, airy room. "Give us that fantastic sound again."

"I— I don't know if we can." Nelson remembered the way Eric's sneaker had tickled his nose. He remembered trying to hold back the sneeze until it grew and grew. "It was sort of an accident."

"There are no accidents!" Drool corrected him. He

63

was wearing a lavender shirt that was opened half-way down his chest. There were at least six gold chains sparkling and twinkling against his tanned skin. "You were meant to make that sound, and we were meant to hear it. You were meant to come with us tomorrow when we shoot the video. You were meant to make that sound again at the end of 'Flat Tire, Full Heart.' "

"Come *with* you?" Eric looked even happier than he had at the Halloween victory party. Quickly, he took his sneaker off and handed it to Nelson.

"To shoot the video?" Nelson could hardly believe his ears. Wait till Lisa Gerchner heard about this! He sat down on the floor, determined to recapture the sneeze. He held Eric's sneaker under his nose and inhaled deeply. Once . . . twice. He took three deep breaths—but nothing happened.

"You've *got* to do it!" Fuzz was pleading now. He laid the Fuzz-guitar aside and faced Nelson, his red silk shirt wet with sweat. "You've got to make that sound again. Nothing else will convey the emotional agony we're looking for. Nothing else will complete the most perfect song I've ever sung!"

Nelson inhaled again. His nose tickled a bit, but still nothing happened. "I just can't do it," he said at last.

"Wait a minute," Eric told him. "Let's try it in the case." He grabbed his sneaker from Nelson and headed for Fuzz's guitar case, still open on the floor. Putting on the sneaker, Eric climbed into the case, leaving a tiny sliver of space beside him for Nelson.

Nelson took one more look around the big, elegant

room. He stared at the three famous rock stars and the glass table still piled with half-eaten cold cuts and cheesecake. Then he looked at the tiny, cramped case. He didn't want to get in, but maybe Eric was right. Maybe it was the only way. Closing his eyes and dreaming of a starring role in Slam's new video, Nelson squeezed into the case beside Eric and shut the top over their heads.

Inside the damp, tiny black space, he found Eric's sneaker once again under his chin. Then as the band began to play the last verse of the song, he felt the throbbing beat of Drool's drums and the jab of Eric's foot against his nose.

"Now your tire is fixed, and you've left too soon," wailed Fuzz, his voice reaching Nelson even through the thick black velvet. "I'm standing here, baby, just breathing your fumes." Nelson inhaled deeply and felt the sneeze building. "Eeeoyoowieee,"sang Fuzz.

"AAAAAAAACHOOOOOOOOOOOO!" sneezed Nelson, as the case popped open and both boys tumbled out again into the bright room. "AAAAAAAA-CHOOOOOOOOOOOOOO!"

"That's it!" Drool was whirling in a mad frenzy around the room. "Wait until they hear that at the studio! Call the junkyard, mates," he yelled over his shoulder into the back room. Two beefy men, even larger than the pair who'd stood guard at the hotel's front door, came rushing into the room and glared at the stowaways. "Tell them we start taping first thing in the morning."

"We do?" Eric, smiling and dazed, massaged his arm to get the blood flowing again.

"What about school?" asked Nelson, feeling a slow, heady triumph when he thought about telling his class that he and Eric were making a video with Slam.

"What about it?" asked Bryan Weird, snapping his fingers. "We'll take care of everything, boys. Don't you worry about school. They can't teach you what *we* can!"

"Meet you at the junkyard at eight o'clock tomorrow morning," Drool told them, shaking first Nelson's and then Eric's hand. "Don't change your clothes, don't change your socks, and above all," he added, clapping Eric on the shoulder, "don't change your sneakers!" Suddenly he looked as if he'd heard something no one else in the room had noticed. He left the boys and sat down at his drums. "Don't change your sneakers," he sang to himself as he thumped the drums with his drumsticks and tapped a pair of cymbals with his feet. "That's it!" they heard him yell as Slam's bodyguards escorted them from the suite. "Come on, mates, I've got a new song!"

As they walked down the stairs between the two brawny men, Nelson and Eric were convinced they were dreaming. Then, when the front door of the Valley Rest Hotel opened and they found themselves back on the street in the middle of Slam's screaming fans, they knew it was all true.

"Hey!" three giggling girls asked them, "what were you doing up there?"

"Yeah," added a boy with braces and a black leather bomber jacket, "how do you two rate?"

The teenagers gathered around them, and Nelson felt more important than he ever had before. "Well," he told them, a happy, proud feeling building in his chest, "we're Slam's technical consultants."

"That's right," Eric agreed. "We do the special effects on their new song."

"You?" The boy with braces laughed.

But the giggling girls pressed closer and sighed. "Wow!" one of them said, looking straight at Nelson until he felt all warm and red under his freckles. "I think you're cute!"

"And if you don't believe us," said Eric, staring defiantly at the boy, "just come to Zeinhoffer's Junkyard tomorrow morning."

"That's right," said Nelson. "We'll be shooting Slam's new video with them. In fact," he added, the proud, tight tingle growing in his chest, "they can't do the song without us!"

The next morning, Nelson and Eric couldn't really tell if any of the kids from the hotel had joined the throng that peered in from outside the metal fence around Zeinhoffer's. First of all, the crowd was much too big to pick out individual faces, and second, the boys spent most of the day underneath the hot, black lining of Fuzz's guitar case.

Drool, the boys learned, was quite a perfectionist and kept asking the band to play the song over until it sounded just right. What they had expected to be an exciting adventure turned into a long, soggy morning. Finally, when the camera crew was drenched with sweat from sitting in the hot sun that bounced off the heaps of wrecked cars, and Fuzz's throat was parched from thirty choruses, and Nelson and Eric had gulped up every last bit of air in the cramped guitar case, Drool was satisfied. The music was right, the words were right, the camera angles were right, and the Slam-bang explosion of emotion that finished the song was perfect. "That's a wrap!" he yelled, jumping down from the bed of the rusty pickup truck where he'd perched his drums.

The video for 'Flat Tire, Full Heart' was finished, and the boys crawled wearily out of their dark, tight prison to receive the applause of the band and crew. "First-rate! First-rate!" repeated Drool, pumping their hands up and down while the relieved film crew clapped and clapped.

"Thanks," replied Nelson and Eric modestly. Nelson started to bow, but as soon as he lowered his head the old familiar smell of Eric's sneaker drifted up, and he felt faint.

"We couldn't have done it without you, mates." Drool took two of the chains from around his neck and handed one each to Nelson and Eric.

"That's right," agreed Fuzz, beaming from under the drops of perspiration that cascaded down his forehead. "Your faces will never appear in the video, and you didn't get in the big dance number or the crowd scene. But just remember, when you listen to 'Flat Tire, Full Heart,' it's *your* song."

Nelson ached all over. He felt tired and dirty and hungry. "Well," he told the band. "So long. I hope your concert's a smash."

"With your help, it's bound to be," Fuzz assured him.

Nelson remembered that Lisa and her brother had probably bought the last pair of Slam tickets in town. "I'm afraid we won't be able to come to the show," he confessed. He glanced at Eric, who shrugged his shoulders and kept massaging his arm. "We couldn't get tickets. You sold out."

Suddenly Fuzz burst out laughing. So did Weird and Drool. All three of them stood beside the old pickup, laughing until tears came.

"Did you hear that?" asked Drool, his heavy hand thumping Nelson on the back. "They think they're going to miss the concert!"

Weird shook his head and wiped his eyes. "Imagine them thinking we would do the show without them!"

"Why?" asked Nelson. "What do you mean?"

"He means we need you for the big finish to our new number," Fuzz told them. "Didn't you know? Now that we've found the right sound, we're going to introduce 'Flat Tire' this weekend."

"Oh." Suddenly Nelson had a sinking feeling. The camera crew was cleaning up the tangled cables, and most of the crowd behind the mesh fence had drifted off.

"Sure," Weird said. "You won't have to worry about tickets. You'll be right up on stage with *us*."

Nelson thought of how much he had wanted to see the concert. Now he wasn't so sure. After all, he could always show his friends the necklace he'd gotten from Drool. "When," he asked cautiously, "are you singing our song?"

"Oh, it'll be the last number," enthused Drool.

"The big finish." He clapped both boys on the back again and handed them autographed pictures. *Rock on* was scrawled across a shiny photo of Slam standing against a brick wall with graffiti splashed everywhere, *from your friends, Fuzz, Drool, and Weird.*

"You're not singing the song until the end of the show?" Eric and Nelson looked at each other, then at the guitar case that yawned open behind them on the steamy-hot concrete.

"Yep. We're saving the best for last," Drool said. "You two will stay hunkered down in your hiding spot until the very last verse. Then, POW! We'll knock 'em dead."

Nelson thought of spending rehearsals locked up with Eric in the guitar case while the stage lights glared overhead. He thought of crawling into the case for the three-hour concert. Of missing the light show and video beamed onto the ceiling, while the pounding of amplified drums vibrated through the hot, black lining of Fuzz's guitar case. He could already feel Eric's foot against his chin and smell the leather sneaker under his nose.

"I'm sorry, Drool," he told his idol. "But I don't think we can make the show."

"What?"

"That's right," chimed in Eric, who must have been remembering the way Nelson's heel dug into his stomach inside the cramped case. "You see—uh, we're going on a trip this weekend."

"Where?"

"Africa," answered Eric.

"South America," announced Nelson.

"How can you do all that in one weekend?" asked the drummer, looking very disappointed.

"We move quickly," said Nelson, edging toward the opening in the junkyard gate.

"Very quickly," added Eric, pushing in front of his friend and racing out of the gate and around the block.

"Wait!" shouted Drool. "We'll introduce the song when you get back."

"No thanks," Nelson told him, stuffing his autographed picture into his jeans and dashing off after Eric. Just as he cleared the long block that contained the tumble of auto parts and old refrigerators, he turned back to stare at the three confused figures still watching him. He waved. "Rock on!" he yelled, then disappeared down the street.

Selma

➤

On Monday after the Slam concert, Peter Newcolm pasted a green slime sticker on Amy Mangione's back while she was checking her spelling test. When she found the sticker, Amy turned around and gave Peter a bloody nose. When she saw Peter's bloody nose, Ms. Tuckman decided to give 6B a new seating chart.

"Little Sylvia Tuckman," their teacher told the class, "*never* got to choose her own seat. Her name began with *Tu* and Harold Traubweiner's name began with *Tr*. That meant she always sat behind Harold. He used to turn around and make the most awful faces at her, but the teacher never saw them. She only saw little Sylvia making them back." Ms. Tuckman sighed. "Little Sylvia spent a lot of time staying after school."

Lisa Gerchner, who was sitting next to Nelson, was too excited about Slam to listen to anyone, even Ms. Tuckman. "I will never," she whispered dreamily to Nelson, "forget this weekend if I live to be a hundred trillion years old!"

Nelson was curious about the show he and Eric had missed. "Did Slam bounce a light show off their chests?" he asked.

"They sure did." Lisa didn't even glance at the chart Ms. Tuckman was drawing on the blackboard. Instead, she leaned toward Nelson's desk and kept on whispering. "Fuzz sang a brand-new love song by Drool. It's called 'Don't Change Your Sneakers.'" She patted Nelson's hand. "I feel totally shattered for anyone who missed it."

Nelson studied the chart that was taking shape on the board. It was covered with tiny X's, and beside each X was a name. He found his name and then he found Eric's. Right beside Eric's name was somebody else's, somebody he had never heard of. "Hayward, Selma," he read to himself.

Ms Tuckman was smiling, the circles on her cheeks stretching into pink pear shapes. "So I've decided to let you all choose where you'd like to sit for the rest of the year." Everyone except Lisa, who was writing FUZZ in green block letters all over her notebook, listened carefully as Ms. Tuckman read the names on the seating chart. "Now, let's see," she said, scanning the board. "Sara and Amy, I'll bet you two would like to sit together. But I can't guess where. Why don't you show us?"

She paused while Sara Kenner and Amy Mangione

looked at each other and giggled. Then, giving little shrieks of delight, they dashed like two playful puppies to the cozy pink rug in the farthest corner of the room.

"What about you, Warren?" Ms. Tuckman asked next. Warren Lansdorf sniffed and looked thoughtfully around the room. His eyes lit up when he saw the snack cupboard. It was only a minute before he and his Kleenex box were settled happily on a pillow by the closet full of crackers, candy, and Fruit Roll-ups.

"Nelson and Eric, I thought you might like to use the hammock from our indoor picnic." Ms. Tuckman pointed to the soft string net that looped across the geography corner.

Nelson turned to look at Eric, who was making a V-for-victory sign with this hands.

"All right!" Nelson grinned at his teacher as the two friends emptied their desks and headed for the back of the room. Together, they took a running start and dove headfirst into the hammock, thudding giddily into a map of South America.

While the boys swayed contentedly back and forth, Ms. Tuckman went on reading the names of all the children in her class. Finally, when Peter Newcolm had built a blanket tent by the window and Lisa Gerchner had traded desks with Ms. Tuckman, they were all sitting exactly where they wanted. "Good," their teacher announced. "Now everyone has a place. Everyone except our new student, that is."

"New student?" Nelson looked at the X next to Eric's name.

"Selma Hayward and her family have just moved to Upper Valley Station," Ms. Tuckman continued. "Tomorrow will be her first day in school, so I think we should pick an extra-comfy place for her, don't you?"

Amy's hand shot right up. "She could sit here with us on the rug, Ms. Tuckman."

"Well, that's very nice of you, dear," Ms. Tuckman told her. "But I had in mind a more special, cozy spot." She folded her pudgy hands and looked straight at Nelson and Eric who were sprawled full-length across their hammock.

Nelson and Eric rolled over on their stomachs to think about it. "It *is* hard coming to a new school in the middle of the year," admitted Nelson.

"But she's a *girl*," protested Eric.

"We *have* got the neatest seat in class," Nelson reminded him.

"But she's a *girl*!" insisted Eric.

"Girls can be all right. A girl plays for the Harlem Globetrotters."

"Okay," agreed Eric. "But if she hasn't got a great dunk shot, she's out."

The next morning, a small, heavy girl who looked almost as round as Ms. Tuckman was standing next to their teacher when 6B filed into the room and took their new seats. "Good morning, everyone." Ms. Tuckman put her arm around the girl, who wore a crinkly blue dress with a big, plastic belt around her waist. "I'd like you to meet Selma."

Eric glowered at Nelson. "If *she* plays basketball," he whispered, "I'm Arnold Schwarzenegger!"

Selma Hayward didn't seem to be nervous about starting a new school so late in the year. In fact, she didn't seem to be worried at all. She folded her plump arms in front of her chest, brushed her short brown bangs off her forehead, and stared at the class. "My father makes more money than yours," she said to no one in particular.

"She might break our hammock," whispered Eric as Selma followed Ms. Tuckman's directions and crinkled over to where the boys were sitting. Her blue patent-leather shoes matched her blue plastic belt, and both made tiny squeaking sounds as she walked.

The hammock dipped very low as Selma heaved her way into the middle of the netting and sunk in between Nelson and Eric. "My house is much bigger than yours," she told them, and then settled down to listen to Ms. Tuckman.

"My handwriting's neater than yours," she said to Eric as the class copied a recipe for butterscotch brownies from the blackboard. Ms. Tuckman had looped her big, curvy script across one whole panel, and Eric needed to use two pages of lined paper to write it all down.

"My notebook has twice as many dividers as yours." Selma opened her big, red three-ring binder right onto Nelson's tiny green one. "And it has a paper punch attached."

"My lunch is better than yours," she told the boys when they opened the paper bags their mothers had handed them that morning. "My mother has my lunches done at a *caterer.*" The hammock swayed as she reached for a white cardboard box tied up with blue-and-white string. While Nelson tried to pick the apple slices out of his yogurt spread and apple sandwich, Selma reached into the box and took out the biggest pastrami on rye the boys had ever seen. Nestled in green paper inside the box were three deviled eggs, a container of coleslaw, and a slice of marble cake.

"Wow!" Eric stopped eating his peanut butter and jelly sandwich. He stared at Selma's lunch. "Are you going to eat all that?"

Selma bit into the pastrami on rye. She turned to Eric with her mouth full and her cheeks puffed out like a squirrel's. "Of course I will. I'm the Deluxe Deli's very best customer."

"Maybe you'll leave one of the eggs," Eric suggested hopefully. He looked longingly at the white box as though he wanted to jump into the green tissue.

"I don't think so," said Selma, munching. "I'm a better eater than you."

And she was. She finished her sandwich, her coleslaw, all three deviled eggs, the marble cake, and half of Nelson's yogurt spread and apple sandwich. Nelson wasn't sure, but it felt as though they were all hanging a lot lower now than they had before lunch. He wondered if Ms. Tuckman was going to make him and Eric sit with Selma for the rest of the school year. He wondered if the hammock would last.

"Well, Selma," he said as the last bell rang and he and Eric got ready to walk home from school, "see you tomorrow."

"I'm smarter than you are," Selma told him and walked off to get her book bag.

The next day was just the same. Only this time, Selma brought *two* cardboard boxes for lunch. She ate everything in both and then polished off the rest of Nelson's avocado and eggplant on whole wheat. "My car is nicer than yours," she said, shaking the last cardboard box to make sure there was nothing caught in the tissue.

"Boy!" Eric folded his arms and glared at Selma. "Your house is nicer. Your car is bigger. Your lunch is better. Maybe you're just too good for us, Selma. Maybe you'd better not share this hammock anymore." He rolled the plastic bag from his peanut butter and jelly sandwich into a ball and threw it into the trash can. "I'll bet you could find a much better place to sit."

"No," said Selma, smoothing the pleats in her plaid skirt. "I like it here just fine. I think Nelson's cute." She studied Nelson's blond hair and freckled face, then grinned. "Besides, he never finishes his lunch."

"You've got to stop giving her your lunch," Eric told Nelson during recess. "Otherwise, that garbage disposal is going to be our permanent hammock-mate."

"I guess you're right." Nelson had noticed a small but threatening tear in one end of the hammock earlier that morning. "It's just that I've never known

78

anyone who liked my mom's sandwiches. It's sort of a miracle."

"It's sort of a pain. You don't want that snobby Selma hanging around all the time, do you?"

Nelson knew he had to do something. Even if it meant eating one of his mother's sandwiches himself. Still, when he finished his whole tofu and cucumber on rye crisp the next day, Selma didn't mind. "That's all right," she told him. "I brought three boxes today. Would you like half a lemon cupcake?"

"Oh, no!" wailed Eric, slapping the hammock and sending it into a tailspin. "I think she *likes* you!"

It was true. Selma seemed to have a huge, mushy, disgusting crush on Nelson. Even when they weren't sitting in the hammock, the new girl made a point of following him everywhere he went. In science class, she asked to be Nelson's lab partner. "My test tube is cleaner than yours," she told him sweetly. In gym class, she sat on his ankles while he did sit-ups. "I can do fifty more than you can," she announced, fluttering her eyelashes and cutting off the circulation in Nelson's feet.

"This has gone too far," Eric warned as Selma prepared to follow them home from school. "If you expect me to give you my Reggie Jackson for your two Dave Winfields, you better ditch Horrible Hayward right now!"

"Sorry, Selma," Nelson told the roly-poly girl when she caught up with them, "Eric and I are going to trade baseball cards. See you later."

Selma looked disappointed, but she waved good-naturedly. "I'll finish my homework before you will," she assured Nelson, turning on her shiny patent leather heels and striding off down the hall.

All that week and all the next, Selma followed Nelson everywhere he went. Her family had moved into a big white house a few blocks from the Malones, so she always met Nelson and Eric on their way to school. Even when they took the shortcut through old Mr. Sheean's rose garden, the boys found her waiting at the end of his driveway. "I had pancakes and ice cream," she'd tell them, smiling. "My breakfasts are better than yours."

In school, she never left Nelson's side. If Nelson turned to page three of his math book, so did Selma. If Nelson decided to eat his lunch with Miles and Eric, so did Selma. And if Nelson raised his hand in English, so did Selma.

"I wouldn't trade places with you for all the lemon cupcakes in the world," Eric whispered while Selma was helping Ms. Tuckman pass out papers. "Not even for all the chocolate ones."

"I know what you mean," answered Nelson. "I've already eaten three beansprout and anchovy paste on wheat germ rounds and two broccoli melts on rye points, and she still won't leave me alone. I don't know how much longer I can last!"

"Why don't you just tell her to take a hike?" suggested Eric, exasperated. "All the guys are teasing you, and our hammock's just about touching the floor."

"I can't be mean to her. My dad says her dad is his new boss and that she can't be as bad as I say and that it's too bad if she is."

80

"Oh."

"And he says we have to go her birthday party, too."

"Her *what*?" Eric sat up straight in the hammock so suddenly that his heels scraped the linoleum floor.

"Her birthday party." Nelson sat miserably in the center of the hammock, his shoulders hunched, his elbows on his knees. "It's this weekend. She called and invited us yesterday."

"Us?" Eric was standing now.

"Yep," Nelson told him. "I said I wouldn't come unless you were invited, too."

"Thanks a lot!" Eric flushed as Selma worked her way toward them from the front of the room. "Well, her father isn't *my* dad's boss, and nobody's going to make *me* go to a dumb girl's birthday party!" He dropped back into the hammock just as Selma plopped down between them. "Nobody!" he repeated, staring across Selma to Nelson.

"I pass out papers quicker than you do," Selma said, crossing her stout legs Indian-style under her green jumper. It had orange trim and a big square pocket with an orange handkerchief sewn inside it. "Are you coming to my party?"

"Hmmmph!" said Eric.

"Don't you want my Eric Davis?" asked Nelson.

"Hmmmph!" repeated Eric.

"And my Darryl Strawberry?" Nelson paused, then stared steadily at Eric and asked in a low, even tone, "How about my rookie Don Mattingly?"

Eric's eyes rounded. "You've got a rookie Don Mattingly?"

"Well?"

Eric considered it. He looked at Selma, then he looked at Nelson. He rolled over into his thinking position and put his chin in his hands. Finally, he rolled back. "Okay," he told Nelson. "But only if you've got a rookie Don."

"I give better parties than anyone," Selma confided on the way home. The two boys walked quickly, trying to keep ahead of her, but she pursued them, sailing down the sidewalk like a small green-and-orange circus tent. "I'm having games, do-it-yourself sundaes, and a magician."

"A magician?" Nelson had saved candy wrappers all last year to collect enough points for the Whammo Magic Kit, a deluxe assortment that included the trick of the disappearing dime.

"And not just any magician." Selma slowed down, huffing and puffing under her violet backpack. "Mr. Presto is coming to my party."

"Mr. Presto? From television?" Nelson loved magic and he never missed "Mr. Presto's Magic Hour" on Saturday mornings. The show really lasted only half an hour, but it was packed with terrific tricks and baffling mysteries. "Mr. Presto, in person?"

"Yep." Selma fell into step with the boys, nudging a space between them with her elbows. "My father had to offer him oodles and oodles of money to get him to come. Mr. Presto doesn't do live entertainment any more."

"I guess he's too busy with his TV show." Nelson began to think Selma's party might not be so bad after all.

"Mr. Presto better be good," threatened Eric, who usually watched the Blazing Battler cartoon show instead of Mr. Presto. "He'd better be great!"

The day of the party, Robin helped Nelson and Eric wrap the Whammo Magic Glove Trick they had bought at the five-and-dime. "I still think you should have bought a Pretty Poppy makeup kit instead," she told them, curling the ribbon on Selma's package with the edge of her scissors. "It has a built-in mirror and compartments for everything." Nelson's sister loved lipstick and eyeshadow and rouge. Whenever she had a friend stay overnight, they would spend hours giggling in front of the bathroom mirror. When they finally came out, they looked like clowns and talked in funny, deep voices that were supposed to match their purple eyes.

"I don't think Selma likes girl-stuff." Nelson taped a pink card onto the package. *Happy Birthday*, he wrote inside it, *from Eric and Nelson.* The outside of the card showed a girl on a swing. The girl didn't look much like Selma, and the swing didn't look much like a hammock, but all the other cards had said mushy things on them, like "to a dear friend" or "with love on your birthday."

"My dress is prettier than yours," said Selma as soon as she opened her front door. Eric didn't pay any attention and brushed past her into the Haywards' living room. Nelson handed her the present. "Happy birthday, Selma," he said.

Selma was crinklier than ever. She was full of pink ruffles everywhere, and her feet were squeezed into black patent-leather shoes. "Thank goodness," she said, when she unwrapped the package from Nelson and Eric. "I was afraid it was going to be another makeup kit." She opened the Whammo magic trick and took out a cape and top hat made of black plastic. She wrapped the cape around her shoulders, fastened the hat's rubber strap under her double chins, and smiled happily at Nelson. "I look more like a magician than you do."

Nelson and Eric were the only children from Ms. Tuckman's class who had been invited to Selma's party. All the other boys and girls were from Selma's old school, and none of them seemed to be paying any attention to the tiny, white-haired man who stood in the middle of the living room waving his hands.

"Welcome to the show," said the old man to all the children at once. He was dressed in a big black hat and a long black cape, and he wore white gloves with little round buttons on them. "I'm Mr. Presto, and I'm here to astound and mystify you."

The little old man didn't look a bit like Mr. Presto. His face wasn't handsome and his stomach wasn't thin. Instead, his shirt front spilled over the wide silk belt around his middle, and deep wrinkles creased the skin near his eyes and mouth. Under the black hat, his pale hair looked limp and scraggly. "Now, if you'll all be seated please," he told Selma's guests in a shaky, thin voice, "I will perform the amazing feat of the vanishing milk."

Most of the children continued to laugh and race around the room, but Nelson and Eric walked up to the old man and stood next to the small, draped

stand in front of him. "Are you really Mr. Presto?" Nelson stared at the magician's wrinkled face and pale blue eyes. "You sure look different on television!"

"Hey, wait a minute," said Eric, who had helped Nelson search through three shoe boxes and an old cookie tin for Darryl Strawberry. "I bet you're not Mr. Presto at all."

The little man stepped back from the stand. "I'll have you know, I am indeed Mr. Presto. I've been Mr. Presto for nearly sixty years." He reached behind the stand and pulled out a purple handkerchief. "I suppose that's part of the problem," he explained. " 'Mr. Presto's Magic Hour' is a rerun."

"A rerun?" Nelson looked confused.

"Of course, dear boy." Mr. Presto took off his hat and wiped his shiny forehead with the handkerchief. "That series was made nearly thirty years ago. I'm an institution."

"You're old." Nelson sat down on the floor and tried to figure out how the handsome, mystifying Mr. Presto could have disappeared without a trace.

"Ah," Mr. Presto said, delighted that someone had finally settled down for the show. "Keep your eyes on this magic wand at all times." He pulled a tiny stick from a shelf behind the stand and waved it three times in the air.

"You're supposed to tap the milk first," Nelson interrupted. "That's how Mr. Presto always does it."

The old man bent over and retrieved a pitcher of milk from behind the stand. Carefully, he set the milk on top of the stand and tapped the wide mouth of the glass. "Ahem," he said, "as you'll notice, this is a perfectly ordinary pitcher of milk."

"The kind you might find on your dinner table tonight," Nelson added.

"Pardon me?" asked Mr. Presto, leaning closer to hear.

"The kind of pitcher you might find on your dinner table—that's what Mr. Presto always says," Nelson reminded the magician. "Every time he does the trick of the vanishing milk, Mr. Presto always introduces it that way."

"Mr. Presto doesn't introduce it that way anymore," the magician told him, looking quite annoyed.

"Oh, yes he does," Nelson insisted. "He introduces it that way every Saturday. Including this very morning while I was eating a Toaster Tart."

"I assure you, young man," replied Mr. Presto, sucking in his stomach and standing very straight, "I do not need your instructions to perform this trick. *I* invented it!" He took the top hat from his head and proceeded to empty the pitcher of milk into it. He waved his wand over the hat and announced, "Now, I will place this hat on my head without spilling a single drop."

"You forgot to say the magic word," Nelson warned just as Mr. Presto lifted the hat and put it on his head. In an instant, the upside-down hatful of milk was splashing over the old man's hair, face, and cape. It rained off the tip of his nose and rushed down his shirtfront onto the draped stand.

"I told you." Nelson smiled knowingly as some of

the boys and girls gathered around the magician, laughing and pointing. "You didn't do it the Presto way."

The little, wrinkled man took the hat off his head once again. From behind the stand, he pulled a bright yellow scarf and began wiping the milk off his face. "The Presto way!" he stormed, shaking out his wet gloves. "Young man, I'll have you know I've been doing things the Presto way since your mother and father were your age. I'm twice as good now as I ever was, and I can prove it!" He drew another prop from behind the stand and placed it on the tabletop. It was a little cage full of white pigeons.

"Oh, yes!" said Nelson. "The trick of the disappearing doves. Don't forget to cover the cage with a white cloth. And then don't forget to say 'Presto!'"

Mr. Presto's face got very red, and he yanked a pink scarf from his stand. "I cover my disappearing doves with a *pink* cloth now," he told Nelson, dropping the cloth over the cage of pigeons. "And, as you'll see, it works very well." He waved his wand in the air and chanted "Abracadabra!" three times in his thin, whiny voice.

"You didn't say 'Presto!'" warned Nelson just as the magician whisked the pink cloth away from the cage. Now the boys and girls around him began to whistle and jeer. All six pigeons remained in the cage, pecking placidly at the bits of grain that were scattered on its bottom.

Mr. Presto's face was redder than ever. "But— but," he stammered, "it *always* works. It *never* fails." He covered the cage with the pink cloth again and almost growled the word *Abracadabra* three more times. Then he tore the cloth off to reveal the cage full of cooing birds.

"There's only one way he'll get those birds to disappear," Eric whispered beside Nelson. "I guess we'd better help him out." He winked and stepped right up to the crowd of boys and girls around Mr. Presto and the pigeons. Before anyone could stop him, Eric had popped open the latch on the cage and all the birds had come flapping out. Six pairs of frantic wings beat the air and circled the room, above the youngsters. Two girls shrieked as the pigeons swooped over their heads and settled in the branches of the living room chandelier.

"Why, why you . . ." Mr. Presto sputtered helplessly as the birds spun above him. "Here, Hilda!" he shrieked. "Come back, Egbert!" But the escaped pigeons didn't pay any attention to him. They continued to spiral and flutter overhead while Selma and her guests clapped their hands in delight below. None of the children could keep from laughing as the elderly magician called each of his pigeons by name. "Here, Cynthia," he yelled toward the chandelier. "Come back, Norman! Gertrude, where are you?"

"I told you." Nelson chortled. "I told you you should have done it the Presto way!"

Suddenly Mr. Presto stopped calling the birds. He adjusted the cape on his shoulders and stared at Nelson. "Ladies and gentlemen," he announced, reaching once more into the draped stand and pulling out a tiny blue bottle. "I think we have time for one last trick. I don't perform this one too often," he told the children. "After all, I'm just a harmless, old, party prestidigitator. But, once in a great while," he added, looking right at Nelson and Eric, "I have an audience that deserves the trick of the transparent troublemakers."

"The trick of the transparent troublemakers?" Nelson tried to remember all the tricks he'd seen on television. "I don't think I've ever seen Mr. Presto do that one."

"Oh, *he* doesn't," Mr. Presto assured him. "He doesn't do it, because he's a very nice, polite young magician. And he knows a lot of perfectly nice, polite illusions." He walked over to where Nelson and Eric were standing, uncorking the blue bottle as he went. "But he doesn't know the tricks I know, you see. I'm afraid the dear man just isn't old enough to have earned a black belt in prestidigitation."

"Is that anything like a black belt in judo?" asked Eric, who backed away when he saw the strange, wild look in Mr. Presto's small blue eyes.

"Not exactly," the magician told him. "But if my two little friends here will act as my assistants, I think I can show you some magic that packs quite a punch." He put his arms around Nelson's and Eric's shoulders. Then he sprinkled blue powder from the little jar over their heads. "Abracadabra!" he said firmly.

"I don't think that's the Presto way," Nelson told him. He was going to suggest that the magician start the trick again when he noticed a strange, empty feeling in his stomach. He looked over to where Eric

90

had been standing, but his friend had disappeared. Suddenly he heard Selma screaming.

"Nelson! Nelson!" His hostess was running around the room, her own black magician's cape streaming behind her. "Nelson, where are you?"

Nelson couldn't understand why Selma was so upset. He was standing right in the middle of the room, right next to Mr. Presto. "I'm over here, Selma," he told her. "What are you making such a fuss for?"

"Oh! Oh, you bad man!" Selma waved a pudgy finger in the old magician's face. "You made them invisible. How dare you spoil my party! You bring them right back!"

Nelson couldn't believe his ears. He couldn't believe the silly way all the children milled around calling his name. "I'm right here!" he insisted as they bumped and pushed up against him. "I'm right here!"

"So am I!" he heard Eric shout. "Stop shoving! Ouch! You're stepping on my toes!"

"Eric!" Nelson shouted back, an eerie premonition tingling along his spine. "Where are you?"

"I told you," Eric yelled. "I'm right beside you, and you're stepping on my foot."

Nelson stared at the empty space beside him. Then he held out his own arm and waved it frantically. Finally, he looked down at the rug where his feet should have been. He saw nothing, nothing at all.

Now Mr. Presto's wrinkled face was full of smiles. He held his cape around him and took low bow after

91

bow while all Selma's guests applauded loudly. "How did you do it?" they begged. "How did you make them disappear? Can you teach us?"

Nelson looked at the magician's smiling, red face. It had a definite shape and a definite place in the room, floating in the middle of the laughing boys and girls. Then, he looked down at his own body. He could feel his arms and his stomach and his legs. But he couldn't see them at all. He had no shape or place. He was nothing. He was zero!

"You bring them back right away!" Selma was the only one not clapping. In fact, she was hopping mad. For the first time, as he watched her scold Mr. Presto, Nelson realized how brave their new classmate was. Brave enough to pretend she didn't care about being so fat. Brave enough to act as though she didn't mind coming to a brand-new school. And brave enough to give the best magician Nelson had ever seen a piece of her mind.

Mr. Presto finally stopped bowing and smiled apologetically at Selma. "It's not as if they didn't deserve it," he told her.

"Oh, they deserved it, all right," Selma agreed. "But if you went around giving people what they deserve, everyone in the world would be invisible!"

Mr. Presto rubbed the stubbly white hairs on his chin. "I guess I got carried away. After all, they *are* fans of Presto's early period, aren't they?" Then, reluctantly, he added, "I suppose I *could* add to my triumph by making them reappear. But I'll need the help of a special assistant if I'm going to manage it." He studied Selma's cape and hat. "You're certainly dressed for the part. Care to give it a try, young lady?"

Nelson covered his eyes with his hands and stared right through them at Selma's happy face. "Why, I'd love to," she said proudly. "What do I do first?"

"Well, first I suggest you make them promise to behave."

"We do!" Nelson and Eric shouted together.

Nelson still couldn't see his friend, but he felt someone step solidly on his right foot. "Ouch!" he said, and then added, "We'll do anything you say, Mr. Presto!"

The magician looked down at his new assistant and winked. "What about Surprising Selma?" he asked. "Do you promise to do anything my assistant requests?"

Selma straightened her hat and tried to look very important. She certainly knew a good idea when she heard one. "Yeah," she said, "do you promise?"

"Yes!" Nelson yelled. But this time he didn't hear Eric beside him. "What about it?" he asked his friend.

"That depends," Eric told him.

"On what?"

"On what Selma wants us to do."

"Walk home with me every day after school," Selma said, folding her arms and smiling in Eric's direction.

"Every day?" Eric's voice sounded wobbly and uncertain.

"Every single day. Except Friday. Fridays Daddy sends a cab to take me to my viola lesson." Selma uncrossed her arms and looked fiercely toward the empty space where Eric and Nelson were. "I play the viola better than you."

"Well, Eric?" Nelson grabbed a chunk of air where he thought Eric's arm should be. It wasn't. He spread his hands out, beating them in circles trying to find a piece of Eric he could hold onto. "I don't know about you, but I sure don't want to spend the rest of my life as the incredible shrinking kid!"

"All right, all right," grumbled the air beside Nelson. "But we get Friday off even when you don't have a lesson."

"Deal!" Selma waddled over to the transparent troublemakers. "Now," she asked Mr. Presto, "what's next?"

"You'll have to say the secret magic word," he told her.

"Okay. What is it?"

The old man beckoned Selma over with one bony finger. "Come here and I'll whisper it to you."

Selma ran over to Mr. Presto and nodded her head as he whispered in her ear, then raced back to the spot where she'd left Nelson and Eric. "You'll have to stand up very straight," she commanded in a serious, grown-up voice.

Nelson sucked in his stomach and held his breath. "Do you promise and swear and hope to have a horrible accident that you'll walk me home from school?" Selma asked.

"We do!" agreed Nelson and Eric, trembling with eagerness to see their own legs and arms again.

"All right, then," said Selma, getting so close Nelson could feel her pink ruffles brush against him. She sprinkled some more of the blue powder into the air and then shouted the secret word right in Nelson's ear. "Presto!" she cried as Nelson felt his limbs tingle and looked down to see his very own hand against his striped shirt. "Presto!" she yelled once more, as Nelson danced in a dizzy, happy circle and watched his own two, solid legs kick for joy.

Flight 942 ✈

No one else in 6B knew why Nelson and Eric began walking Selma home after school. None of them had been invited to Selma's party, and none of them heard how Mr. Presto had made the two boys invisible. "If you ever tell anyone that we were saved by a crummy girl," Eric threatened Nelson, "I'll stop being your best friend."

So Nelson and Eric simply told their class that Selma wasn't really too bad after all, and they turned out to be right! Selma stopped boasting and, after a while, she was hardly better than anyone at anything anymore. She even made new friends and didn't need to follow Nelson around. Still, walking home with her had definite advantages—like the after-school snacks she always kept tucked in the pencil bag tied to the lining of her backpack. "Here," she'd say, grinning generously, "I think I have just enough cupcakes to go around."

"You know," Nelson told Selma one afternoon as the three of them dug into the mini-mousse cups she passed out on the way home, "I sure will miss you during Christmas vacation. I'm going to my grandmother's for a whole week, and all she ever has for snacks are carrot sticks and raisins."

"Raisins aren't so bad," Selma consoled him. "I had some in my iced oatmeal cookies yesterday." She licked the inside of her mousse cup clean, then unstuck her chewing gum from the cup's clear bottom and popped the pink wad back into her mouth.

"Well," admitted Nelson, "it's not just the raisins. I wish someone I knew was going to be with me."

"You know your grandmother!" Eric, who had finished his mousse too, was using the cup to collect bottle caps. "She'll be with you."

"I mean on the plane," Nelson told him. "I'm flying to Phoenix all by myself."

"Hey, that's great." Eric stopped to dig up a green bottle cap with the heel of his sneaker. "My mom won't let me fly by myself. You're lucky."

"Maybe. Only I keep wondering why the airlines charge less for kids. Do they only give you half a seat?"

"Airplane food," Selma said, "comes in little tiny packages. My mother never lets me ask for thirds. I'd love to go on a plane by myself, Nelson."

But Nelson wasn't sure. As vacation got closer and closer, he got less and less sure. And finally, two days after Christmas, as he and Robin piled into the back of the car for the drive to the airport, Nelson decided air travel wasn't as safe as everyone seemed to think. "What if the pilot forgets where Phoenix is?" he asked the back of his father's head. "What if he gets lost and has to take the long way and runs out of fuel?"

Mr. Malone didn't turn around, but he looked into the backseat through the rearview mirror. "They have a flight engineer on board, Nelson. It's his job to study the charts and know just where the plane's going at all times. He goes to school and is specially trained."

"What if he went to the wrong school?" Nelson felt Robin staring at him. "And in case anybody thinks I'm scared," he added, "I'm not."

"Nobody cares," remarked Robin, who, it turned out, was looking out the window and not at her brother. "Pennsylvania."

"It doesn't count," Nelson told her. "I wasn't looking. Besides, I already called Pennsylvania."

"When?"

"Yesterday, when we went to the shoe store."

"That's not fair. You and Mom went to the shoe store. I wasn't even there."

"So what, dum-dum?"

"So I quit. That's what."

"Thank goodness," their mother said from the front seat. "The end of the great license plate war.

Now maybe you two can relax and look at the beautiful scenery instead of the traffic."

"Robin only quit because she knows she'll lose," observed Nelson.

"Did not, warp-brain. I've got twelve states, and you've only got five."

"Six, counting Pennsylvania." Nelson studied the new shoes he'd gotten for the trip to his grandmother's. They were brown loafers, and they felt all tight and hard on his feet. "Besides, I would have won anyway. Just think of all the license plates I'll see out west."

"I wouldn't miss Harriet Wiley's overnight for all the license plates in the world," Robin told him. "We're going to put sparkles in our hair, and Mrs. Wiley's going to teach us how to do eye shadow."

Nelson tried to wiggle his toes the way he did in his sneakers, but there wasn't even enough space to tell which toe was which. "I don't see why I have to be the only one to go to Grandma's," he said. "I thought Christmas was supposed to be a family holiday."

"It is," agreed Mr. Malone. "But sometimes there's just not enough family to go around. You know I have to go see Uncle Al. He's very sick, and Aunt Hannah needs my help right now."

"And the only reason I offered to stay home with Robin," Mrs. Malone told him, "was because Grandma and Grandpa are convinced you're old enough for a private visit. They were sure you'd love flying out on your own."

"What if," Nelson asked as the car nosed its way through the winding tunnel to the airport parking lot, "the flight engineer gets caught in a traffic jam on his way to work, and no one has extra copies of his maps?"

"I think they keep extras in the glove compartment." His mother laughed.

"What if," Nelson asked as he helped his father unload his suitcase from the trunk and carry it into the terminal, "the flight engineer went to a different school than the pilot did, and they start fighting about how to fly?"

"I think that's why they have copilots," his father told him. "They're sort of like referees."

"What if," Nelson asked as his mother and father and sister walked him up to the little doorway where Great West's flight 942 was boarding, "we have to fly through a snowstorm, and the windshield wipers don't work?"

"It's a beautiful day," his mother told him, kissing him gently and tucking his boarding pass into his pocket.

"What if," Nelson asked as the airplane headed toward a runway and he looked out the window at his family who waved gaily and got smaller and smaller, "there's a dangerous hijacker on board?"

"Everyone's luggage has been x-rayed," the flight attendant told him as the plane lifted off the ground. "Even yours."

"I only packed that stuffed puppy because my grandmother gave him to me." Nelson scrunched against his seat as the tall, blond woman opened a tray onto his lap. She was wearing a bracelet with three tiny gold airplanes hanging from it.

"That's nice," she said. "Now, would we like a snack?"

Nelson checked the seat next to him, but it was empty. He wondered who the flight attendant was talking to, but then he remembered Miss Belinda, his kindergarten teacher. Miss Belinda always said "we" whether she was talking to the whole class or just one child. "We can't have such a noisy choochoo during naptime, Nelson," she used to tell him. "This is quiet time. Let's put our choochoo into the station, so it can rest, too."

"My name is Miss Enid," the flight attendant told him, making her red lips into big, fat shapes when she talked. "And I'm going to be our special friend on this flight." She handed him a paper book with a picture of an airplane on the cover. *Airways to Adventure*, it said in big letters that filled the sky. *A Coloring Book for Wee Travelers.*

"I'm too old for coloring books," said Nelson.

"We're under twelve, aren't we?" asked Miss Enid, her airplane bracelet jingling. "Everyone under twelve always gets the Wee Travelers' Fun Kit." She reached above her to a cupboard and took out a box of crayons.

"I'm eleven and a half. Don't you have a movie I could watch?"

Miss Enid looked pale. "Flight 942 to Phoenix," she said defensively, "features deluxe three-abreast seating, free in-flight snacks, and roomy overhead luggage compartments. But NO movies." She patted Nelson on the head and her color came back. "I'll go get our snack." She bustled off down the aisle and left Nelson to stare out the window.

First he looked up. There were no birds. There were no clouds. Then he looked down. There were no buildings, no people or cars. There wasn't even any ground. In fact, the whole window was filled with a gray vapor that left Nelson wondering where the ground ended and the sky began. It was like being stuck in the middle of a big wool sweater with only one sleeve off and your head covered.

"Here we are," sang Miss Enid suddenly. Nelson noticed she'd put on a big blue apron with an airplane on the pocket. She set a glass of milk on his tray, and beside it, she put a little box that looked like a circus wagon.

"I'm too old for animal crackers," he told her. He looked around the cabin at the other passengers. "Why can't I have a cheese danish like everybody else?"

"This is part of the Wee Travelers' Fun Kit," Miss Enid told him, looking hurt. "Wee travelers love animal crackers." She knelt beside him in the aisle, the airplane on her apron pocket disappearing into folds of blue. "They also love to play games. Would we like to play I Packed My Suitcase and Flew to Phoenix?"

"I— I don't think so." Nelson studied Miss Enid's face to see if she was going to cry. He was surprised to see that she was smiling, a big, wide smile that showed a little bit of red lipstick on one tooth.

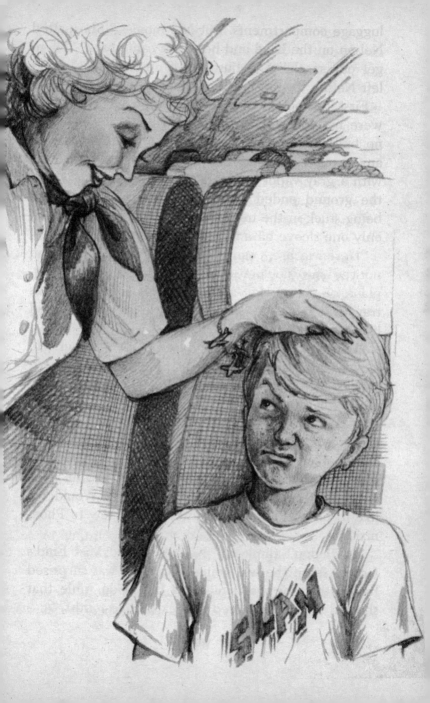

"Of course we want to play," she said as though she hadn't even heard him. "We're just afraid to start, that's all. But don't worry, Miss Enid will go first." She cleared her throat and sat back on her shiny black heels. "I packed my suitcase and flew to Phoenix," she announced in a voice so loud that several passengers turned around. "And in it I put my favorite stuffed puppy to sleep with."

Nelson shrunk into his seat. "I told you," he said, "I only brought that puppy for my grandmother."

"And what did we pack next?" asked Miss Enid cheerfully.

"I have to go to the bathroom."

"Are we going to play the game just as soon as we come back?"

Nelson looked at Miss Enid as she stood up. She was very thin, with long, slender arms and legs. She could probably run pretty fast if she took off her high heels and, he was certain, she knew every inch of the plane. "Okay," he sighed. "We'll play just as soon as we get back."

Nelson took as long as he dared in the tiny bathroom, flushing the deep blue water down the toilet three times and washing his hands twice. Unfortunately, Miss Enid was waiting beside the door when he came out. "I packed my suitcase and went to Phoenix," she said. "And in it I put—"

"What's that?" interrupted Nelson, pointing to a small door at the end of the aisle.

"Oh, that? That's just the cockpit."

For the first time since he'd been aloft, Nelson looked interested. "You mean where the pilot flies

104

the plane?" He remembered what his father had told him. "And the flight engineer and the referee?"

Miss Enid laughed. "Yes, Captain Hendricks and his flight crew control the plane from the cockpit. Would we like to see it?"

"Would we!" Nelson could hardly believe that anything as neat as a look inside a real, live cockpit could be included in the Wee Travelers' Fun Kit. "We'd really like that, Miss Enid. We'd like that a *lot*!"

The flight attendant looked very pleased to see Nelson so enthusiastic. "Well, all right," she said, taking him by the hand to the front of the plane and knocking on the tiny door. "I'll just bet the captain would love to show us how he makes this great big plane play peek-a-boo with the clouds."

A tall, barrel-chested man turned to greet them. There was still a small piece of cheese danish clinging to his brown mustache. "Captain Hendricks," Miss Enid announced, "this is Wee Traveler Nelson Malone. We wanted to meet you."

"Hello, Nelson," said the captain in a nice, natural voice. He didn't sound like he was talking to a Wee Traveler. He sounded like he was talking to a perfectly normal, almost-twelve-year old. "I'd like you to meet my copilot, Harold Archer, and my flight engineer, Dick South."

"Hello." Nelson nodded toward the two men the captain had introduced. But he barely saw them. He stared instead at the huge dashboard behind the Captain's seat. It was filled with buttons, dials, and a blinking computer screen.

"Where's your joystick?" asked Nelson.

"I beg your pardon?" Captain Hendricks looked confused.

"There has to be a joystick," Nelson told him. "Your cockpit looks exactly like the control console of Transatlantic Ace. It's just about the most awesome video game in the world." Nelson, who had broken 3,000,000 on the Space Challenger machine at Gino of Genoa's Pizza Palace and whose name was up as high scorer on all but two games at the Upper Valley Station bowling alley, knew a good video game when he saw one.

Captain Hendricks smiled. "Well, Nelson, I guess these three power throttles are as close to a joystick as you'll get on a 757." He pointed to three levers, one for each of the plane's engines.

"Wow! Three joysticks!" Nelson's fingers itched to close around one of the levers. "I bet you're terrific at dodging enemy aircraft and low-flying clouds!"

"I'm glad to report that we don't encounter enemy aircraft too often," the captain told him. "As for low-flying clouds, I usually let our automatic pilot handle that."

"Automatic pilot?"

"Yes, Nelson. When visibility is poor, I can program our flight computer to take over."

Nelson was disappointed. "In Transatlantic Ace, you have to remain alert at all times. You never know when the Dashing Destroyer or Tailspin Teddy will dive at you out of the sky. They can destroy you with one laser blast."

But Captain Hendricks seemed to have lost interest. He turned his back on Nelson and bent over the U-shaped handle of the control column in front of him.

"In fact," continued Nelson, anxious to explain the fast action and excitement of his new video favorite, "it's not only other planes that cost you points. There are weather factors to consider, too."

"Ohhhh," said Captain Hendricks.

"That's right. There's tropical storm Angina and whirlwind hazards and lightning bombs."

"Ughhhh," groaned the captain, slumping across the column as Miss Enid rushed to his side.

"Well, it's not as bad as all that," Nelson reassured him. "Because you get two extra lives every time you explode Angina or Tailspin Teddy."

"Captain! Captain!" Miss Enid yelled. "Speak to me." She shook the captain's shoulders and then raced over to the flight engineer who had also fallen forward in his seat. "Oh, my goodness, they're not moving. They're sick!"

Now Nelson realized that something was indeed terribly wrong with the flight crew. He glanced at the copilot, whose face had turned fish-belly gray. "What's wrong, Mr. Archer?"

"My stomach!" groaned the copilot, clutching his middle. "I think I've been poisoned." Now he, too, began to pitch forward, and Nelson felt the plane dip as Archer's head flopped onto a row of dashboard buttons.

"You can't be poisoned," protested Miss Enid. "I haven't even served lunch yet. The only thing you've had to eat is the snack, and, after all, I had the same cheese danish you did. As you can see, I feel . . ." Suddenly she stopped talking and put her long, red-polished fingernails against her forehead. "Woozy," she finished, collapsing into a small seat by the door. "Very woozy."

Nelson couldn't believe how quiet and green the bouncy flight attendant had become. Her big arms and legs had folded in on themselves, and she was moaning quietly. "The passengers," she whispered, looking helplessly toward Nelson. "They—they all had the danish, too."

"Oh-oh." Nelson opened the small door and peered cautiously down the plane's aisle. Sure enough, all the men and women on board were slumped forward in their seats, their noses in plates of unfinished cheese danish. Nelson walked out into the cabin and began searching every seat for someone who wasn't green or moaning. Finally, he found a dark-haired woman in a seat over the wing. She was looking out the window and munching on a piece of danish.

"Excuse me, ma'am," he said, touching her sleeve gently. "I don't think you should finish that danish."

"Oh?" She turned to look at Nelson. She had a pretty face and a nice smile. "Do you want a bite?" She broke off a bit of the pastry and held it out to him. "Here you are, honey."

"Uh, no, thank you," he said as she took back the piece and popped it into her mouth. "You see, everybody who's eaten that danish is very sick, and—"

"Nonsense!" said the pretty lady. "I feel perfectly . . ." She stopped speaking as the familiar gray-green color drained the blush from her cheeks. "Awful," she continued in a soft, surprised voice. "I feel perfectly awful." She folded her arms on the tray in front of her and put her head down, knocking a plastic cup of coffee into the aisle.

Nelson took a last, desperate look around the cabin as the plane took another sickening lunge downward. It was clear that he was the only Wee Traveler on board, and that everyone else had eaten the lethal pastries. He left flight 942's passengers groaning softly into their trays and raced back to the cockpit.

Just as he crossed the threshold, the plane dropped again and sent Nelson, three plastic plates, and an orange safety vest skating across the floor right into Captain Hendricks' seat. "Ughhhh," said the captain.

"Excuse me, sir," replied Nelson, relieved to find the pilot awake. "Don't you think now would be a good time for the automatic pilot?"

"I—I tried it." The captain's head hung heavily against his chest. "It's out of order, and I can't keep control much longer." He gripped the control column in front of him so tightly that his knuckles turned white, but suddenly he was too tired to try any more. As Nelson watched in horror, the captain's hand slipped away and fell limply to his side. "It's up to you, now." He gurgled and then lay still as stone while the whole plane dove, falling through wispy clouds that flew by outside the cockpit window.

"It's up to me? I—I haven't even seen the maps."

Nelson glanced at the flight engineer who was curled in a corner, his teeth chattering. "I don't know where we're going."

The flight engineer stopped chattering and raised his head. It wobbled dangerously, as if it were too heavy for his neck. "Call the tower," he managed to gasp before his head rolled back onto his chest.

"But I didn't go to flight school," protested Nelson, shaking the engineer's shoulders. "I can't even drive a car!"

"You didn't eat the cheese danish," mumbled the copilot from his seat near Captain Hendricks. "You're our only hope. Punch that green switch and grab the captain's earphones. Then . . . Then . . ." But Nelson never heard what to do next, because Archer fell so far forward that he tipped out of his chair and lay stretched, full-length and deadly silent, across the floor.

Nelson swallowed hard, then reached for the green switch. "I *did* get to the seventh level of Transatlantic Ace," he told himself. "And I *did* beat Michael Mason's high score even though he had a home-game version and got to practice every day." Slowly, he eased the headphones off Captain Hendricks and punched the switch.

"Tower to 942. Tower to 942." Nelson heard a voice crackle to life inside the headphones he was holding. Quickly, he put them over his ears and slipped into the copilot's seat. "Do you read us, Great West?"

"Malone to tower," Nelson said into the mouthpiece that fit under his chin. "I read you." Then he remembered something he had heard on television. "Loud and clear," he added.

"What's going on up there?" asked the crackling voice. "You've changed direction four times. Who do you think you are, the Red Baron?"

Nelson took a deep breath and told the voice the whole story. How Miss Enid had passed out cheese danish and how everyone had passed out. How he was their only hope, but he was eleven and a half and, even though he was pretty terrific at Transatlantic Ace, he wasn't too sure about 757's.

For a few seconds, the tower didn't say anything. Then Nelson heard a long, low whistle in the headphones. "Wow!" the voice said. "We've got trouble. You're headed straight for a Phoenix twister."

"A what?" Nelson peered out the window, but he saw nothing. Nothing except the same cloud wisps the plane had been flying through ever since Captain Hendricks had lost control.

"It's a storm, 942," the tower explained. "We call them twisters because they can twist an airplane in half."

Nelson grabbed the control column and stared out the window again. The clouds were moving faster now, and the whole plane seemed to be hanging in the sky at a crazy angle, so that he had to fight to keep himself from careening into the dashboard. Suddenly he thought he saw another airplane spinning like a top in the distance. It was flying very much the way the Dashing Destroyer always did just before he closed in for the kill.

Instinctively, Nelson reached for a power throttle.

111

It looked just like the joystick he always used to dodge the Transatlantic Ace's archenemy. "Oh, no, you don't!" he cried, yanking back on the throttle, making certain the small black plane had moved out of sight before he released it. Slowly flight 942 seemed to right itself and Nelson's head snapped back from the controls.

"I don't know what you did," the tower reported gleefully, "but you just avoided a major collision. Great flying, ace!"

"Thanks." Nelson kept his eyes glued to the plane's window. "Now, if I could just find Tailspin Teddy, I could get an extra life."

"Sorry," crackled the tower. "I don't copy."

"I wouldn't try, if I were you," Nelson warned. "It's pretty hard unless you've played before." As he was talking, his eye caught a blur of movement outside the window. Off to the left, he saw Tailspin Teddy closing in on the 757. His plane was monstrous, dwarfing the Great West jet. The sun glinted off its wings, nearly blinding Nelson as he reached for the dashboard dial that matched the gas gauge in Transatlantic Ace. Deftly, he maneuvered the control column until Tailspin was just within radar range.

At the precise moment that he thought he could see the gleam in his enemy's eyes, Nelson pulled another throttle all the way down as sharply as he could. Tailspin Teddy dropped from sight below the window, and the tower cheered. "You're magnificent, 942! I've never seen a jetliner perform an aerial maneuver like that last stunt of yours. I

don't know who you are, but I sure am glad you're aboard!"

"So far, so good," admitted Nelson, scanning the sky. "But we still have to deal with tropical storm Angina." Squinting, he stared into the distance and, sure enough, dead ahead he spotted a distant cluster of black clouds. They were whirling themselves into a tight, dark ball and rolling straight toward the plane. Without a second's hesitation, Nelson pushed the control that looked like the bomb hatch in Transatlantic Ace. He pushed and pushed and, just as it seemed the black cloud-ball was going to swallow flight 942, he dove underneath it and swooped toward a patch of blue sky. "That's two extra lives!" he yelled. "What's next?"

"That's 200 extra lives," the tower corrected him. "You just saved everyone on board, 942. Congratulations. Your next move is to land that crate and, after what you've just accomplished, gliding down that runway should be a snap. Now, listen carefully."

Nelson did. He pushed every button the tower told him to and, as the big plane lowered slowly, he steered straight down the middle of the yellow markers. It was the same way he'd landed the Transatlantic Ace's plane countless times before. He let up the flaps and dropped the wheels, and flight 942 lumbered onto the tarmac and raced toward a cheering crowd that had gathered outside the airport's main arrival gate.

Tugging at the brakes just as he'd been instructed, Nelson nosed the plane toward the gate and removed his headphones. He leaped over the bodies of Captain Hendricks and his crew, pushed aside Miss Enid's long legs, unlocked the cockpit door, and found himself blinking in the Arizona sunlight.

"Hooray!" A shouting group of men and women charged up the stairs that had been pushed over to the door. Some of them were carrying cameras and microphones. "Hooray!"

"How does it feel," asked a short, heavy man who was the first to reach Nelson, "to save a jetliner?" The man stepped back as a doctor with a black leather bag rushed past him into the cockpit. Then he shoved a microphone with KWAT written on it under Nelson's nose.

"Well," began Nelson, "I . . ."

"Where did you learn to fly like that?" asked a second reporter, who leaned over the back of the first to stick another microphone in Nelson's face. "Did you know you're a hero?"

Nelson looked back inside the cabin and was glad to see Captain Hendricks sitting up beside the doctor. "All I did was play a video game," he told the reporters, looking over their heads to see if he could find his grandmother in the huge crowd behind them. "It wasn't even my best score."

"The kid acts like it was nothing! Did you hear him?" A skinny, blond woman with a television camera pushed her way to the top step. She pointed the camera first at Nelson and then inside the cabin at Captain Hendricks, who was shaking his head and smiling weakly.

"I sure did," said the captain, struggling to his feet and limping out the door to stand beside Nelson. "It may not have been your best game, young man. But you saved the day. We all owe you our lives. Here, take this." He looked down and unpinned the pair of silver wings he wore on his uniform. He stuck the pin into Nelson's Slam T-shirt and put his arm around him. "You deserve to wear Great West wings," he said, choking with emotion.

"And you deserve this, too," said a voice from the crowd. A silver-haired man in a blue suit handed Nelson a red velvet box. Inside, resting in a shallow, velvet hole that just matched its shape, was a golden key. "I'm Mayor Phillips," the silver-haired man explained. "And this is the key to our city. We're proud to welcome you to Phoenix."

"I'm only here for a week," Nelson told him. Then, smiling with relief, he waved to the tall, slender woman who strode up the stairs behind the mayor. "Grandma!"

"Thank goodness," his grandmother said, reaching across the mayor to hug Nelson. "You had Grandpa and me very worried. I'm afraid I've burnt the turkey."

"Grandma, I'm glad you told Mom and Dad to let me fly by myself. It was a really neat trip."

"That's nice, dear. Hurry and grab your things before the light meat gets any darker."

Nelson ducked into the plane and ran to his seat. He scooped up his suitcase, the box of animal crackers, and the *Airways to Adventure* coloring book. On the way back, he met Miss Enid, who was wobbling down the aisle beside the doctor. "We had lots of

116

fun," he told her. "We're going to be sure to fly Great West from now on. Good-bye."

Before Miss Enid could answer, he had slipped out the door and back to his grandmother, who grabbed his arm and pushed her way through the crowd of reporters. "They certainly make a fuss, don't they?" she grumbled, fending off a photographer with her purse. "Oh, Nelson!" She looked eagerly at the little box in his hand as they headed for the parking lot. "You even brought cookies. Can I have an elephant?"

"Sure, Grandma," said Nelson, handing her the wagon-shaped carton, then peering into the sky as a giant jetliner zoomed overhead. "You can never be too old for animal crackers!"

Florinda

————————————————➤

The flight back to New Jersey wasn't nearly as exciting as the trip to Phoenix had been. Even though Nelson flew Great West again, he didn't get to see the cockpit, and not a single passenger was sick—unless you counted Nelson himself, who ate six bags of peanuts and wished he hadn't.

"How was Arizona?" asked Eric and Selma when Nelson joined them in the hammock the day after vacation.

"It was okay." Nelson looked around as if something were wrong. "Wait a minute. Did somebody fix our hammock? We're not sagging so much anymore."

"Maybe it's not the hammock," Selma told him. "Maybe it's me. My parents put me on a diet the day after Christmas."

Nelson noticed now that Selma's eyes had lost their defiant sparkle and that her cheeks weren't quite as round as they had been ten days before. "No more catered lunches?"

"No," said Selma, miserably. "Nothing but low fat yogurt and celery sticks."

"No after-school snacks, either?"

"Nope." Selma opened the brown bag she had on her lap and let Nelson peek inside. "This is what my mother gave me for the science trip today. How am I going to get through a whole museum on two Fig Newtons and a carton of cottage cheese?"

"Not a whole museum," Eric corrected her. "Mr. Bigsley says we're covering just dinosaurs today."

"I don't care what we're covering," Selma insisted. "I just wish we were covering it with Ms. Tuckman. I don't think science teachers stop for ice-cream breaks."

"Dinosaurs?" interrupted Nelson. "I thought we were touring the planetarium today."

"It's closed for repairs," explained Eric. "And Mr. Bigsley can't get the bus for another day."

"I hope that doesn't mean the gift store is closed, too." Selma looked hopeful. "They sell candy bars there. And little gumdrops shaped like Tyrannosaurus rex."

"Don't worry, Selma." Nelson grabbed his own paper bag and followed his two friends to the end of the line the class had formed at the door. "You can share my havarti and prune whip sandwich."

"Sure," added Eric, "you can have one of my hard-boiled eggs. You can even have the dessert my mom made. I don't know what it is, but it's red and it wiggles."

On the bus trip to the museum, Selma polished off Nelson's sandwich and both her Fig Newtons. Once they were inside the dinosaur wing, Mr. Bigsley was so busy discussing the Mesozoic era that he never noticed Selma devouring Mrs. Lerner's red dessert. Then, while the class toured the stegosaurus and brontosaurus displays, Selma stayed at the end of the line so she could finish her cottage cheese and Eric's egg. By the time they got to the pterodactyls, she was eyeing Nelson's bag of stone-ground taco chips.

Nelson, who used to be crazy about dinosaurs when he was little, had a hard time paying attention to Mr. Bigsley while he fought to keep his taco chips. "Selma," he asked, popping the last three into his mouth at once, "donth you think you've had enuv?"

"These huge, birdlike creatures," Mr. Bigsley told them, "were actually reptiles. When fully mature, they had a wingspan of as much as fifty feet." He spoke very slowly, because he was reading from a metal sign on the front of a display. He had planned to talk about Venus, so he didn't have anything prepared on dinosaurs. "Because of its extreme weight," he continued reading, "the cumbersome pterodactyl probably did not fly very high, but took advantage of low wind currents to drift from precipice to precipice of its rocky dwelling."

While Selma grabbed his taco chip bag and wolfed down the crumbs that had gotten stuck in its corners, Nelson studied the pterodactyl display. It featured a huge father pterodactyl with its wings open above a nest. It looked as if the beast were just coming in for a landing, his gigantic talons spread wide to dig into the crevice where the nest was sheltered. Waiting for him was a mother pterodactyl, her wings folded in a huge V across her back, and a baby pterodactyl with its sharp, greedy beak open for the food that dangled from father's mouth.

"I'm hungry," announced Selma, looking longingly at the wide, open beak. "Let's go to the gift store. The gumdrops are on me."

"All right!" Eric slapped his empty pockets and followed Selma. "Come on, Nelson."

But Nelson had found something a lot more interesting than gumdrops. "You go ahead," he told them, bending over a plastic stand filled with pterodactyl eggs. "I'll catch up." Fascinated, he reached out and touched one of the tiny, fossilized balls. It was black and hard as a rock. It was hard to believe that inside, curled up forever, was the frozen embryo of a flying dinosaur that, if it could have come to life, would grow wings bigger than his living room! "How did pterodactyls become extinct?" he asked, picking up the black ball and turning it over in the palm of his hand.

Mr. Bigsley squinted at sign after sign. "It doesn't say," he admitted at last. "Scientists are still arguing about why the Mesozoic era ended. I guess the museum doesn't want to choose sides yet."

"Well, I sure wish dinosaurs hadn't disappeared," Nelson said, tossing the ball from one hand to the other in little loops. "I'd much rather have a ptero-dactyl for a pet than a hermit crab."

"Hmm. I'm not sure your mother would feel the same way." Mr. Bigsley took off his glasses and put them in his shirt pocket. "I'm afraid, children, that's all the signs there are—uh, I mean we've run out of time. Let's get back to the bus. Nelson, put your ball in your pocket and let's go."

Nelson looked at the tiny egg. Then he looked at Mr. Bigsley.

"Nelson!" the science teacher barked. "You heard me. Put that thing in your pocket and march!"

Nelson did. All smiles, he dropped the little ball into his pocket and joined the line of chattering children that moved toward the museum exit. All the way back to school, he kept reaching into his pocket to touch the smooth, shiny egg. All the way home, he kept opening the pencil case in his backpack to make sure the little ball was still there. And, as soon as he got safely home, he ran upstairs to his bed-room, took out the egg, and put it into the terrarium next to his hermit crab, Horatio.

"You can't keep it," Eric told him. He watched Nelson's hermit crab scuffle toward the egg, try to sit on top of it, and fall down its smooth sides. "It's a valuable fossil. You've got to take it back."

"Do not."

"Do too."

Nelson stooped to retrieve the egg. But Horatio, who had now managed to get his tiny claws around it, wasn't giving up easily. Nelson pulled and the little crab pulled, and finally, Nelson came away with the egg in his hand. "Do not," he announced firmly.

"All I know," Eric told him, "is that thing is older than Mr. Glendinny, and if we don't get it back to the museum, we could be in for a lot of trouble." He grabbed the egg from Nelson and headed for the door.

"Hey! That's mine!" Nelson ran after Eric and tried to pry his friend's fingers open from around the fossil.

"It is not yours. It belongs to the museum." Eric hid the egg behind his back, while Nelson lunged forward, tackling him around the waist and sending both boys to the floor in a heap.

"Now look what you've done!" Nelson watched the egg roll out of Eric's hand and wobble toward him across the bedroom rug. He picked it up and examined its shiny, black shell. "It's cracked!"

He was right. As the two boys silently studied the egg, there was no denying the uneven zigzag that traced its way down one whole side of the fossil. "Gee," said Eric solemnly, "I guess when you're older than Mr. Glendinny, you crack pretty easily."

"I can't take it back now." Nelson rolled the egg over in his hand and then gently laid it back inside the terrarium. Now that there was nothing left to fight about, he and Eric decided to shoot baskets behind Brian Kenley's garage. When he came home, Nelson noticed that Horatio had finally managed to scale the egg and was perched on its top, his two front legs wrapped possessively around the fossil.

The crack in the shell seemed wider than ever, and Nelson decided it would be best to leave the egg where it was.

After dinner, Nelson was hard at work on a paragraph about the class trip. He had just written *The museum we toored is a tresure of knowlege* when he heard a strange sound coming from the terrarium he'd hidden under his bed. He got down on all fours and peeked under the bedspread. Again he heard the sound—a tiny, distant tapping, as if someone miles away were building a house.

Except that the noise wasn't coming from miles away. It was coming from Horatio's glass bowl! Nelson stuck his whole head under the bed and stared at his hermit crab. He was nose to feelers with Horatio when the noise started again. Clearly, the little crab had nothing to do with the peculiar, rhythmic *tap-tap-tap*s that kept repeating in the quiet twilight of his bedroom.

Tap. Tap. Tap. The sound was definitely coming from the black egg, which seemed to be spinning in place, slowly and precariously working its way across the sandy bottom of the terrarium. *Tap. Tap. Tap.* Nelson watched Horatio wave one feeler and then sidle over to the side of his bowl. *Tap. Tap. Tap.* The crab began digging furiously. *Tap. Tap. Tap. Tap.* Horatio quickly covered himself in the sand, digging down until only the tiniest sliver of his brown shell was left above the surface. Even though you couldn't see them, Nelson guessed that Horatio had very sensitive ears.

Tap. Tap. Tap. Nelson stared as the black egg

rocked gently back and forth, making tiny ripple marks in the sand under it. *Tap. Tap. Tap. Tap.* It was almost like the Mexican jumping beans that Mr. Hollings sold at the five-and-dime. Nelson knew that tiny bugs trapped inside the beans made them wiggle and snap. But what could be living inside a 150-million-year old egg?

All night long, the gentle tapping continued. Nelson finished his museum paragraph and got into his pajamas, but the tapping didn't stop. When his mother came in to kiss him good-night, he talked very loudly so she wouldn't hear the busy sounds in Horatio's bowl. "Good night, sleepyhead," his mother said.

"GOOD NIGHT, MOM," yelled Nelson.

"Sleep tight. Don't let the bedbugs bite."

"WHAT BEDBUGS?" yelled Nelson. "THERE ARE NO BEDBUGS IN HERE. HONEST."

His mother looked bewildered as she tucked the covers around Nelson and headed for the hall. She paused in the doorway, her shadow slanting across the room like a giant, flat gingerbread cookie. "Remind me to call Doctor Wilson tomorrow," she said. "I think we'd better get your ears checked."

Tap. Tap. Tap. Long after his mother had closed the door and gone downstairs, long after he should have been asleep, Nelson listened in the dark to the distant construction sounds under his bed. *Tap. Tap. Tap.* And, next morning, when a chunk of sunlight finally worked its way under his window shade and into his eyes, he could still hear the same strange noise. *Tap. Tap. Tap.*

"What if," asked Nelson at breakfast, "an egg was left alone for a very, very long time and then it cracked and started making tapping noises?"

"Nelson, are you doing another science project in your room?" Mrs. Malone stopped dishing out scrambled eggs and looked searchingly at Nelson. "Because if you are, keep in mind that your father is allergic to anchovies, fur, and feathers." Now she resumed piling the eggs onto the plates in front of her. "You remember what happened with your hamster experiment, don't you?"

"If he doesn't, *I* do," said Mr. Malone, taking a plate of eggs and passing it to Nelson. "I sneeze just thinking about it."

"But, Dad," insisted Nelson, "if you hadn't chased Florinda, she wouldn't have bitten you."

Nelson's father took his own plate and began spreading his eggs on toast. "I wouldn't have chased that hairy monster if she hadn't decided to move into my sneaker. Even after you took her back to the pet store, I couldn't get through a set of tennis without breaking into a rash!"

"Florinda was very talented." Even though he'd only been allowed to keep her two weeks before Mr. Malone's sneezing got out of control, Nelson remembered his furry ex-pet with affection. "I'll bet she's the only hamster in the world who could run an exercise wheel backwards."

"Big deal!" Robin had taken the top off the ketchup bottle and was smothering her eggs in ketchup. "Rinaldo can do that, and he's only a mouse."

"The only talent ratty Rinaldo has," observed Nelson, "is taking naps." He stared at his sister, who was already on her second helping of eggs. "You have ketchup on your nose."

Robin rubbed her nose with a napkin, spreading the tiny dot of ketchup into a big, red smear. "My mouse has character and class, and he's a lot more intelligent than that boring old hermit crab of yours. Horatio's so dumb he can't even squeak!" She rubbed again, spreading the ketchup smear across her left cheek. "And he doesn't even have a tail to chase!"

Mr. Malone hadn't taken a single bite of his breakfast. "Please," he asked, sneezing into his napkin, "could we stop talking about hamsters and mice and—and . . . achoooo!" He sneezed again, dabbing his teary eyes with a fresh napkin. "It's a good thing for Rinaldo that he started out tiny, pink and hairless. And that he stays in his cage now that he's fat, white and shedding. As for whatever you're hatching in your room, Nelson, it's got to—to . . . achoooo! . . . go!"

Even though he had no idea *what* he was hatching in his room, Nelson decided his father was right. He'd better get it out *soon*. After breakfast he packed the tapping egg in Kleenex and put it carefully into his backpack. As soon as he got to school, he told his hammock-mates about the strange noises the egg was making. Eric was worried, but Selma was delighted. "You're hatching a chick, Nelson. Just think! A little pterodactyl of your very own!"

"How will it get out?" Nelson thought about the

pecking sounds and about the way the crack had been growing wider and wider. "That egg's as hard as a rock."

"It *is* a rock," Selma corrected him. "On the *outside*. But who knows what it's like on the inside? Maybe it's been waiting all this time to get nice and warm. Maybe when your hermit crab sat on it, the nice, cozy feeling got through the crack."

"What'll I do?" Nelson touched his backpack protectively. "Where will I keep it?"

Selma looked around the room. She saw the classroom pets resting comfortably in their cages—the iguana dozing, a patch of sunlight dappling its scales; the squirrel monkey, chattering happily while it crumpled someone's math paper in its paws. "I think we should tell Ms. Tuckman," she said at last. "She likes animals, and she's great at keeping secrets."

Nelson felt the small lump the egg made in his backpack. He knew that, if he put his ear close enough, he would hear the familiar *tap-tap-tap*ing. He thought about the strange creature that might be doubled up inside, pecking at the inner layer of the eggshell. There weren't many grown-ups who could be trusted with something so miraculous and wonderful, but Ms. Tuckman, he decided, was one of them.

"Why, that's the most astounding, terrific, amazing thing I've ever heard," his teacher told him when the three children brought the egg to her after school. She held it next to her ear and smiled her faraway little Sylvia Tuckman smile. "Yes! Yes! There's definitely something in there that wants to get out." Then her little Sylvia smile disappeared, replaced by a serious, grown-up frown. "Of course, we can't keep it here. Mr. Glendinny would be bound to find out. We're going to have to take it to Mr. Bigsley."

"Mr. Bigsley!" Her three students looked at one another. "But, he'll make us take it back."

"Nonsense." Ms. Tuckman wrapped the egg back in its Kleenex and handed it to Nelson. "If I know Ed Bigsley, he'll want to hatch it himself! When it comes to animals, there's simply no one better qualified to be a mother hen. Come along." Tying the strings of her purple bonnet under her chin, she led the children out of school and into the center of town.

Three blocks past the five-and-dime, they turned onto a small, winding street with neat, white houses up and down its length. They walked up the driveway of the fifth neat, white house they came to and rang the bell. Mr. Bigsley, a fat gray kitten in his arms, answered the door. "Ed," Ms. Tuckman said as soon as they were ushered into the science teacher's living room, "grab a seat because I don't think you should hear this standing up."

Mr. Bigsley and the gray kitten settled into a flowered chair by a big bird cage. The tiny cat didn't seem interested in the cage at all, but the huge green-and-red parrot inside couldn't take its eyes off the kitten. "Cat got your tongue?" squawked the bird, cackling at the kitten. "Cat got your tongue?"

"Oh, stop it, Copernicus," scolded Mr. Bigsley. "If you're not quiet, I'll cover your cage."

130

"Bad kitty!" screeched the parrot, as the kitten curled up and went to sleep on Mr. Bigsley's lap. "Better get the kitty litter. Shame on you!"

"Wow!" Nelson loved the big bird's sharp tongue and brassy plumage. "I'd love to have a bird like that!"

"I think Copernicus is one of a kind," Mr. Bigsley said. "But I know where you could get a nice, well-behaved parakeet who says perfectly harmless things like 'Time for a song' and 'Birdie go night-night.'"

"No, I can't. My dad's allergic to anchovies, fur, and feathers," Nelson said, sounding pretty sorry for himself. "That's why we're here." Then he told the teacher about the egg and how it had started tapping. He explained that he was very sorry he'd taken it, but now he had to think of some place to keep it until it hatched. While he was talking, a shaggy, red-haired spaniel bounded into the room and started chewing on the laces of his sneakers.

"Down, Einstein," commanded Mr. Bigsley. "Dinner's not for an hour."

"Boy, you really *do* like animals!" Selma sat down on the sofa, next to Ms. Tuckman. "Here, Einstein," she called. The friendly dog galloped over to her and put his furry paws in her lap. Giggling, she let him cover her round face with sloppy dog-kisses.

"Yes, I do," admitted Mr. Bigsley, stroking the sleeping kitten. "But I'm afraid I haven't had too much experience with prehistoric ones. In fact, I've never heard of anything so remarkable in all my life!" He watched as Nelson unwrapped the egg. Carefully, Nelson held the black treasure up to the light so the science teacher could get a better look. Suddenly, as the heat of the light warmed the egg, the tapping sound that had seemed so distant grew louder. *Tap. Tap. Tap.* Nelson felt the round fossil rock back and forth in his hand and everyone in the room, even Copernicus and Einstein, stopped to listen. *Tap. Tap. Tap!*

"Look out!" Eric, who had been standing beside Mr. Bigsley, backed away from Nelson. "It's coming out!"

Sure enough, as everyone stared in fascination, a tiny green claw kicked its way through the crack in the egg. Nelson, a wonderful, tingly feeling working its way up from his feet, cradled the egg in both hands and watched as the first little claw was joined by a second. "Get a towel!" he heard Ms. Tuckman shout. Selma and Eric scurried into the kitchen while Nelson sat on a chair, the egg in his lap. "Boil some water!"

Einstein cocked his red head to one side and whined as a purple wing followed the green feet out of the egg. Mr. Bigsley made a tiny sucking sound, and Copernicus covered his head with his wings. *Tap! Tap! Tap!* Suddenly, the crack split wide open and the egg broke into two halves that tumbled off Nelson's lap onto the floor. There, perched on Nelson's right knee, sat the most wonderful, scaly, slimy baby pterodactyl imaginable. It looked up at Nelson with shiny, red eyes and opened its yellow beak wide. "Awk!" it said, plaintively. "Awk!"

"Oh, my gosh!" Eric stared as the tiny monster

132

spread its pointed wings wide and begged Nelson for food. "It thinks you're its mother."

"A perfectly natural bonding reaction," commented Mr. Bigsley, whose voice sounded excited and shaky. "The first object a newborn chick sees after it comes out of its egg represents the warmth and security of motherhood."

Copernicus whistled in amazement as the ungainly chick made its way up Nelson's leg and nuzzled his sweater with its head and beak. "Awk! Awk!" it pleaded.

"What can we feed it?" asked Nelson. Gingerly, he reached out and stroked the green scales on the pterodactyl's back. He felt all warm and wonderful as the ugly little reptile rubbed against him. "It's okay, Florinda," he said gently. "We're going to get you something to eat."

Selma sighed. "Oh, what a beautiful name!"

"I just knew she was a girl," approved Ms. Tuckman.

"I think you should call him Tyrone the Terrible." Eric was the only one who sounded disappointed.

"Nope," insisted Nelson. "My mind's made up. I'm naming her after a very talented, humble hamster. I think they would have liked each other." Nelson looked at the snapping yellow beak in front of him and imagined the two pets coming face to face. "Unless Florinda II decided to eat Florinda I," he added thoughtfully.

"Here we go," said Mr. Bigsley, bustling back into the living room from the kitchen. "Copernicus loves these." He handed a box with a picture of two para-keets on it to Nelson. The parakeets were touching heads and in the heart shape under their beaks, it said, "Happy Bird Treats . . . Because your bird needs a song in its tummy!"

Nelson turned the box over and poured some Happy Bird Treats into his hand. Before he had righted the box, Florinda was pecking at the tiny pellets with her beak. Again and again, she dipped her head and scooped up the food, tickling Nelson's palm. Finally, when the whole box was empty, she folded her purple wings over her back, turned three times in Nelson's lap, and then fell asleep in a nest she'd shaped in his sweater.

Nelson didn't dare move. He was too happy. He just held his breath and watched the shiny green dinosaur snore peacefully, her beak resting gently on his leg. He didn't care if he never owned a dog or a cat or any other pet for as long as he lived. Florinda was all he wanted. And it was clear she felt the same way. From the minute she woke and Nelson was finally able to stand up and walk around, the little pterodactyl followed him everywhere.

If Nelson went into the kitchen to help Mr. Bigsley, so did Florinda. Flopping her clumsy wings, she either hitched a ride on his shoulder or padded after him on the floor like a loyal puppy. Whether Nelson walked upstairs to look at his science teacher's rock collection or downstairs to the basement pool table, Florinda didn't let him out of her sight. When it was time to go, both of them were brokenhearted.

"But she can't sleep without me," protested Nelson when Mr. Bigsley suggested he would build a nest for Florinda in his bottom dresser drawer.

"Nelson," Ms. Tuckman reminded him, "you know you can't take her home. And you also know we can't afford to let anyone else find out about Florinda."

"That's right," Mr. Bigsley agreed. "I once told the local chapter of Finchfinders about Copernicus, and they sent an ornithologist out to tag him. Next, they wanted a bird doctor to examine him, and then they suggested I 'lend' him to the chapter for further study. I nearly lost him for good."

"But I don't think she'll eat unless I feed her." Nelson looked lovingly at Florinda who waddled over to him and pecked his sock with her long beak. "Awk!" she said adoringly.

Finally, though, Nelson admitted he had no choice and agreed to let Mr. Bigsley care for Florinda. Still, every morning during the weeks that followed, he always made sure to rush over to the little white house to feed her before school. And, every afternoon, as soon as school was over, he ran back to watch her take her afternoon nap and give her dinner. Each time he saw her, Nelson noticed that his pet had gotten bigger. She was just as affectionate as ever, of course, but pretty soon her head came up to his waist and she had outgrown the dresser drawer.

"I'm thinking of transferring her to the garage," Mr. Bigsley told Nelson one afternoon. He adjusted the glasses on his long nose and studied the huge bird in Nelson's lap—or half in Nelson's lap. Florinda was already ten times as big as she had been when she hatched, but she insisted on acting like a newborn chick whenever Nelson visited. She would spread her wings and rush toward him, then beg him to sit down so she could roost in his lap.

"But she likes to look out the bedroom window," Nelson objected, stroking Florinda's scales. Often, when he walked in, he caught the pterodactyl staring silently through the glass at the open sky, as if some ancient instinct were calling her to try her wings in the low-flying clouds she saw scudding by. "She'd hate the garage."

"I don't know what else to do, Nelson." Mr. Bigsley shook his head. "She's growing so fast. She's already too big for the giant economy size of Happy Bird Treats and, when she opened her wings yesterday, she knocked over two tables and a lamp."

Nelson looked at Florinda, who had now wandered over to the window and was staring wistfully at a flock of birds that wheeled overhead. She *was* gigantic, he had to admit. She was already a lot bigger than Einstein, and Mr. Bigsley said that, as far as he could tell from the reading he'd been doing, she'd soon be as big as a small house. They *would* have to find a way to keep her safe and happy and far from prying, curious people. But how?

Suddenly, as if in answer to the loud whistles from the birds outside, Florinda spread her mammoth wings and knocked over Mr. Bigsley's night table. She flapped her wings up and down, sending two paper-thin purple scales drifting to the floor. "What's she doing?" Nelson rushed to his pet's side and tried to calm her by scratching under her chin.

But it was no good. Florinda obviously had an itch Nelson couldn't scratch. Again she beat the air with her wings. Turning once toward Nelson, she opened her beak. "Awk!" she said, then looked back toward the window and finally, with a huge, desperate lunge, broke through the glass and lumbered off into the sky.

"Oh, no!" Mr. Bigsley raced to the broken window and shaded his eyes, trying to follow the heavy pterodactyl's jagged path above the house. "She wants to join the flock. She's going to fly with them!"

"She can't!" screamed Nelson, watching Florinda flapping gamely after the last bird in the formation, which now began to move off toward the center of town. "We've got to stop her!"

Nelson grabbed a handful of Happy Bird Treats. He and Mr. Bigsley rushed out the door just as Selma and Eric were coming in. "Hurry!" yelled Nelson over his shoulder. "Florinda's loose!" Without a word, the two friends turned around and raced out of the house, too. Together, the four stumbled into the street, their eyes fastened on the row of tiny dots that streaked across the sky and the one immense, bobbing shape that flapped after them.

"It's worse than we thought!" yelled Mr. Bigsley, puffing from exhaustion as they moved with the flock toward Main Street. "Those are pigeons she's following. They're headed for city hall!"

Sure enough, the black dots formed a V that

zoomed straight for Upper Valley Station's municipal building, circled a few times, and then broke up to settle like pepper all over the roof above city hall's glistening white columns. Helpless, Florinda's four friends watched her join them, landing behind the last pigeon with a thud that shook the whole roof. As the rest of the flock cooed quietly and settled down to roost, the newest member marched directly to the clock tower and began pecking at the big hand. "Awk!" she screeched, nudging the hand from four to five. "Awk!"

The oversize pigeon couldn't go unnoticed for long. Soon, a huge crowd had gathered beside Nelson and the others. "Oh, my goodness!" Mr. Bigsley poked Nelson and pointed to a tall, bald man. "What did I tell you? That's Herb Warner, the president of the Upper Valley Station Finchfinders. He's the most relentless bird-watcher I know!"

Nelson looked at the bald man. The bald man looked at Florinda, then wrote in a lined tablet. "Yes," he told the people around him. "No doubt about it, that's a purple-winged grosbeak." He scribbled furiously once more, then snapped the tablet shut. "The largest specimen I've ever seen!"

A woman behind Nelson held her toddler up above the crowd. "Look, Angela," she told the child. "Look at the big birdie."

"That thing's a menace," said a tall man beside Mr. Bigsley. "We have enough trouble with all those pigeons. Think of the damage a giant like that could do."

"Yeah," agreed someone in the crowd. "My taxes helped pay for that buiding."

"I got here as soon as I could," whispered another voice, very close to Nelson's ear. He turned around to find Ms. Tuckman, her purple bonnet ties streaming, in the thick of the crowd. "We've got to get Florinda away from them before they do something they'll be sorry for later!"

Nelson watched Florinda teetering on the roof. She had started nudging the little hand across the clock face. "Awk!" he heard her call. He dug into the bottom of one of his pockets, and his fingers closed gratefully around four small pellets.

Ducking out of the crowd, he signaled his teachers and Eric and Selma. Soon, Florinda's five friends were gathered on a little grassy plot by the flagpole. Nelson held the treats high in the air above his head. "Here, Florinda!" he called as loud as he could. "Here, girl!"

Florinda turned her huge head to one side and studied the group of familiar humans with one red eye. Then, her beak open, she flapped her wings and, as the crowd below yelled, soared into the sky over their heads.

A short, well-dressed man rushed over to Nelson. The Finchfinders' president rushed after him. "Excuse me, young fellow," said the short man. "I'm Mayor Fenster. Just what do you know about this bird?"

Nelson looked helplessly at Ms. Tuckman, who looked at Mr. Bigsley, who looked at Herb Warner, the Finchfinders' president. "Absolutely nothing," Mr. Bigsley said firmly, shaking his head. "What bird?"

"What bird?" asked Herb Warner. He laughed and pointed to Florinda, whose huge shadow was blocking out the sun. "Why, that incredible, phenomenal, historic specimen up there. That's what bird!"

"Oh," said Mr. Bigsley, pretending to notice the pterodactyl for the first time. "You mean that green-crested nuthatch?"

"Green-crested nuthatch?" Herb Warner looked flabbergasted. "That's not a green-crested nuthatch, you fool. That's a purple-winged grosbeak. And probably the largest ever sighted, too."

"Sorry." Mr. Bigsley put his hands in his pants pockets and whistled a little low whistle, as if he couldn't have cared less. "That's a perfectly ordinary, run-of-the-mill green-crested nuthatch." He stopped whistling and stared up at Florinda, who seemed to be coming in for a landing. "Oh, a trifle larger than usual, I'll admit. But otherwise, a completely common type. I've seen hundreds myself."

"You have?" Herb Warner seemed crestfallen.

"Oh, yes indeed. Isn't that right, Sylvia?" Mr. Bigsley turned to Ms. Tuckman, who smiled at the president.

"Why, yes," she assured him. "This specimen is nothing special. I've seen several much larger."

"You have?"

"My good man," Ms. Tuckman told him, stepping back as Florinda zoomed down to the flagpole's base and began nibbling at a pellet in Nelson's palm, "these birds are all over the state. Where have you been? Open your eyes!"

Mr. Warner didn't look convinced. "I still think we should have it banded," he insisted, his eyes wide as he took in Florinda's tiny, paddle-shaped tail and her tooth-lined beak. "Just in case."

"I think you're right," announced Nelson, handing Florinda a second pellet as Mr. Bigsley and Ms. Tuckman and Selma and Eric looked at him in amazement. "In fact, that's just what we're going to do," he added, winking at his friends, "if we can find a way of getting this specimen to Finchfinders headquarters."

Mr. Warner stepped back to examine Florinda, who already seemed larger than she had when she escaped. "Yes," he said, chewing on the tip of his pen. "There *is* a transport problem."

"Why not use the bookmobile?" suggested Mayor Fenster, pointing to a large white van parked by the library. "After all," he added, studying Florinda's red eyes and sharp, green talons, "if this *isn't* a green-crested whatever, I want people to know that it was spotted in Upper Valley Station."

"Of course," agreed Ms. Tuckman, who suddenly understood what Nelson was up to. "In fact, we have a special stop planned right after the Finchfinders." She turned and winked as broadly as she could at Mr. Bigsley, then turned back to the mayor, her cheeks shiny with mischief. "We're going to take this specimen straight to the zoo and order a plaque honoring the sharp-eyed citizens of Upper Valley Station."

"Yes! Yes!" approved Selma, smiling at Eric. They had both caught on to Nelson's game now, too. "We're going to contact the press and the media and let everyone know how our mayor helped capture a green-crested, purple-winged whatever!"

"Well, well!" The mayor beamed as Eric used another Happy Bird Treat to lure Florinda toward the white van with a book painted on it. Out of the book were pouring all kinds of storybook characters—Snow White, Robinson Crusoe, elves, witches, even a dinosaur.

Nelson sighed with relief when he saw the picture of the brontosaurus on the side of the van. "Look, Florinda," he told the pterodactyl, "a friend of yours." He pointed to the brontosaurus and tapped the van's metal wall.

Florinda turned her head to the side and studied the picture. Finally, she seemed to recognize it, because she ambled right up to the white truck for a closer look. When she did, Nelson crawled into the back of the van with the last pellet of Happy Bird Treat. "Here, girl," he called softly. "Come on in." He held his breath as the huge reptile poked her head through the open door, winked at Nelson with one red eye, and scrambled up into the van.

"Let's go!" Eric raced toward the door, slamming it behind Nelson and Florinda. Then he and Selma piled into the backseat behind Mr. Bigsley and Ms. Tuckman. As Mr. Bigsley started the engine, Mayor

Fenster, President Warner, and the rest of the crowd gathered around the van.

"I'll meet you at Finchfinders headquarters," Mr. Warner shouted above the sputtering motor.

"Fine." Mr. Bigsley nodded and smiled, then backed the van out of the library parking lot.

"And I'll meet you at the zoo," the mayor yelled. "Just as soon as I've notified the press."

"Yes, indeed." Ms. Tuckman waved gaily as the van drove off, and Florinda and her friends headed out of town.

They were speeding along the highway when Nelson finally calmed Florinda and poked his head into the front of the van. "You're not really going to the Finchfinders, are you?" he asked.

"Of course not," Mr. Bigsley answered without turning around. "We're taking this specimen straight to the Pinelands. It's the only place in New Jersey we can hide Florinda. She'll thrive if we set her loose there."

"Set her loose?" Nelson felt a big lump in his throat and heard his own voice sound strange and wobbly.

"It's the only way, Nelson. I've read up on pterodactyls. My hunch is they lived by the ocean and the Pinelands are full of wetlands and marshes that would make perfect nesting sites for Florinda. There are over a million acres where she can fly and soar and explore."

"And best of all, Nelson," added Ms. Tuckman softly, "she'll be free of mayors and newspapers and ladies with curious babies."

144

"I guess so." Nelson looked down at Florinda, whose beak was resting in his lap. He stroked her ugly neck and fought to see her through his tears. "It's just that I . . ." He felt the huge beak nip one of his shirt buttons playfully. "It's just that I love her."

"That's why you have to let her go," said Ms. Tuckman as the van left town and headed toward the highway. She smiled at Nelson. It wasn't her little Sylvia Tuckman smile, but it wasn't a serious grown-up smile either. It was somewhere in between, and Nelson couldn't help smiling back.

They drove for several hours before the van bumped its way down a dirt road and finally stopped at the edge of a tree-lined swamp. "This should be perfect," Mr. Bigsley announced. "Eric and Selma, open the back door, please."

Florinda hopped out of the van almost immediately. Her wings opened as she sniffed the damp air. She waddled over the sandy soil and splashed accross a shallow channel. There, wedged between two scrub pines, she found a little nest of grass and leaves. She turned around three times, then settled comfortably into the nest as if she had always lived there.

"But she'll be all alone." Nelson watched the friendly misfit rustle her wings and peck a bug off the leaf of a bright pink orchid. "She's the only pterodactyl in the world."

"The only one we *know* of, Nelson," Ms. Tuckman reminded him. Then she added gently, "It's time to go now."

Sadly, Nelson walked toward the nest, while the others waited silently by the van. "Well, Florinda," he told his pet. "I hope you won't be too lonely."

"Awk!" said Florinda, rising in the nest to nuzzle Nelson with her beak. "Awk! Awk!"

That was when Nelson made a wonderful discovery. There, underneath Florinda, centered in the grassy nest, was a small black ball. Brushing the tears from the corners of his eyes, Nelson stared at the hard, rocklike egg. Carefully, tenderly, he picked it up and rolled it over in his hand. It was exactly like the egg he'd taken from the museum, the egg from which Florinda herself had been hatched!

Nelson felt so happy, he let out a little yelp for pure joy. "Awk!" he cried, hugging Florinda around her neck. "Awk!" he yelled, leaping down from the rock and running back to the van. The lump in his throat was gone as Mr. Bigsley started the engine. There wasn't a tear in his eyes as the van backed out from the swamp and pulled away. That's why Nelson knew he wasn't mistaken. That's why he was perfectly sure, as he watched her from the back of the speeding bookmobile, that Florinda was waving one huge purple wing good-bye.

MEET THE GIRLS FROM CABIN SIX IN

Coming Soon

MY CAMP MEMORY BOOK

Fans of *Camp Sunnyside Friends* and campers everywhere will be thrilled with this inviting album, ideal for preserving favorite camp memories.

Don't Miss These Other Camp Sunnyside Adventures:

(#7) A WITCH IN CABIN SIX   75912-8 ($2.95 US/$3.50 Can)

(#6) KATIE STEALS THE SHOW   75910-1 ($2.95 US/$3.50 Can)

(#5) LOOKING FOR TROUBLE   75909-8 ($2.50 US/$2.95 Can)

(#4) NEW GIRL IN CABIN SIX   75703-6 ($2.50 US/$2.95 Can)

(#3) COLOR WAR!   75702-8 ($2.50 US/$2.95 Can)

(#2) CABIN SIX PLAYS CUPID   75701-X ($2.50 US/$2.95 Can)

(#1) NO BOYS ALLOWED!   75700-1 ($2.50 US/$2.95 Can)